Texas rancher Case Mars. *Harley after a crooked pa* *New Orleans socialite Sa* *the run from the mob—or .... stop. Their worlds couldn't be less compatible or their attraction more high-octane…but there are dangers and shocking secrets to battle before they can dream of a future together.*

Be Mine This Christmas
Texas Charm
Texas Magic
Be My Midnight Kiss

Lone Star Lovers
Texas Heartthrob
Texas Healer
Texas Protector
Texas Deception
Texas Lost
Texas Wanderer
Texas Bodyguard
Texas Rescue

Texas Danger

Texas Heroes: The Marshalls
Book Three

Jean Brashear

© Covers by Rogenna
sweettoheat.blogspot.com

Formatting by BB eBooks:
bbebooksthailand.com

This one's for Tommy.

Chapter One

The road to hell sure had been more fun than this one.

So why had he given up the sweet life of no strings, hot women and his Harley?

Oh, yeah, right—his damn fool notion to save the Flying M Ranch he'd gladly left behind so long ago.

But not for Black Jack Marshall's sake. His father was gone, and no one was shedding tears over the loss. Wiley Cantrell, however, deserved better. He'd been more a father to Case than Black Jack ever had, but he was only the foreman. The ranch was in the hands of the son Black Jack had hated, and the old man was probably spinning in his grave over that.

So here Case was, driving a big rig, the only one left from his grand notion of diversifying. He'd been well on his way until he'd made one crucial mistake: trusting a smooth-talking stranger who'd helped him get a loan the local bank couldn't extend.

Then vanishing one day with nearly every dime Case had put together to save the Flying M. Now Case was back where he'd started, nearly dead broke and itching to be anywhere but here.

He had another option: his obscenely wealthy cousin Josh Marshall, a big star in Hollywood, who'd probably loan him the money.

But he'd never ask. Not after the way Black Jack had given the finger to his whole family in his teens. Case had only met Josh and his brother Quinn a couple of times as a kid, but from what he knew, their whole branch of the family was solid and upstanding—the exact opposite of his dad.

Black Jack would have asked for the loan in a heartbeat.

But Black Jack would never have paid it back.

Case might have his own checkered past, but he was not his old man. He'd long ago lost count of the fights they'd had, the beatings he'd endured. Finally, it had been easier just to leave. Scary as hell to be alone at sixteen, but it beat battling his old man until one of them wound up in the hospital—or worse.

But forget Black Jack. Wiley had left a message asking Case to get home as soon as he could. He'd said they might have a lead on Case's cheating so-called partner. Case hoped to hell Wiley was right. He itched for revenge, though he was the fool who'd trusted too easily.

But first he needed fuel. And coffee. He turned into the Lazy J Truck Stop and pulled up to the pump.

Samantha St. Claire was exhausted. The terror she'd barely held at bay in New Orleans had preyed on her mind every mile she'd driven, running for her life.

For the lives of her family.

She'd hoped to find her Uncle Roland in San Angelo as promised in the cryptic letter that had sent her serene, orderly life into free-fall—but her favorite relative had vanished, and now she had no idea what to do or where to go. Only that she couldn't go home.

She'd been warned.

Uncle Roland was the black sheep of her mother's family,

but he'd always doted on her, and she'd thought his days as a scoundrel were long over.

Apparently not. His misdeeds couldn't include something simple like sleeping with the wrong man's wife or drinking too much, though—oh, no.

He'd gotten himself right in the crosshairs of the biggest crime boss in New Orleans. Even Samantha, with her patrician family background and her staid job as a banker, had heard of Etienne Gascoigne. She would never have dreamed, however, that their paths would have any reason to cross—but she'd learned better. His men had come for her. Had vividly demonstrated that her social standing meant absolutely nothing. Had forever robbed her of the ability to feel safe.

And they'd threatened her family. If she breathed a word of what she'd learned, what she'd endured that terrifying night would be nothing to what they would do to her dignified father, her beautiful, fragile mother or her two beloved sisters.

What was she going to do?

She'd fled New Orleans in haste, withdrawing only the paltry sum she could take from an ATM. Raised to be her father's princess and a leader of New Orleans society, however, she'd made a rookie mistake that first day in handing over her credit card without thinking—then asking for it back too late.

One of her attackers had shown up in the parking lot of the cheap motel that night.

Her red Porsche was far too noticeable—another mistake. She'd rectified it by climbing out the bathroom window of the motel that night, and she'd faced the fact that her precious car had to go. In Houston, she'd traded it in—and lost her shirt on it—for the distasteful but anonymous sedan she'd hoped would last long enough to get her to Uncle Roland.

Wherever he was.

But she'd been too frightened to battle over the cost. Her situation had rapidly become deadly serious, and all that had mattered was getting away from the men who were after her. She couldn't contact the authorities; she couldn't ask her family for help. It didn't matter that she had no experience with subterfuge, that this shadow world she'd entered was light years from all she'd known.

Until she found her uncle, she was on her own. There was no one to turn to, no one to trust.

But now that junker car wouldn't start. She'd left it a mile down the road from this truck stop and hiked here to buy herself time to think.

"Hon, you sure you don't want to eat something? You need some meat on those bones, and you look dog tired," said the waitress named Jolene. She'd been refilling Samantha's coffee cup for the last hour as she took up space in a booth she had no right to monopolize.

But she didn't know how far her scarce funds would need to stretch. How she would ever find more—an irony when she had ample savings in addition to a trust fund.

"I'm okay. Thank you. I-I guess I should—" *Go*, she was about to say.

But Jolene's attention had shifted to someone headed that way.

"Well, look what the cat dragged in!"

Case was headed toward the back corner to grab his favorite booth when he realized somebody was in it.

His favorite waitress, Jolene Burnett, spotted him and broke into a grin. "Out kinda late for an old man, aren't you?" It was typical of her to remember his recent thirty-second birthday. The irony of Jolene—at sixty plus a few she wasn't counting—calling him an old man, wasn't lost on Case.

"Darlin', I'm still young enough to kiss you breathless, but come over here and let me make sure."

"Oh, no, cowboy, I'm too hot for the likes of you. You here for a shower first or a meal?"

"You gonna wash my back?"

"Sugar, you just keep hoping." Her helmet of aerosol-laden bleached-blonde hair hardly moved as she shook her head at him, dimples winking.

"You sure play hard to get, Jolene. A guy could get discouraged."

Despite the late hour, her eyes still twinkled. "Get on with you. Grab yourself a stool, and I'll be right there."

"They're full. How much longer—" He leaned around to see who had his booth.

Whoa. Hold the phone, folks. The night just got a whole lot brighter.

Samantha was already frowning when the man peered around Jolene.

Dieu, a man shouldn't be so gorgeous. That black, black hair falling down over his right eye and curling slightly on his neck, the play of muscles in his forearms. The long, lean thighs, the wide shoulders, the cocky once-over he was giving her...a player, clearly. Samantha rolled her eyes and looked away—but not before he caught her.

His dark eyebrows rose in challenge.

She gave him her mother's best *you-are-beneath-me* dismissal, something she herself was normally far too well-mannered to do.

But nothing was normal. Life was too frightening. Too serious for a flirt like him.

Jolene turned to her. "Hon, are you about finished?"

Guilt assailed her. "I am so sorry. I've been here too

long."

"I don't mind sharing," the man said. "Don't get up."

She grabbed her purse and started to rise, anyway.

Jolene's hand on her shoulder stopped her. "You look far too exhausted to be driving. At least have something to eat. Would you mind if Case here sits with you? I promise you he's harmless."

"Low blow, Jolene. You are gonna ruin my reputation, talking like that."

"Oh, get on with you. Sit down and behave yourself."

But to his credit, he hesitated, addressing himself to Samantha. "It's your decision. If it helps, I can't stay long, anyway. Just refueling, then I gotta get back on the road. My rig's still got miles to go."

She could have a reprieve. They were in a crowded café, after all. What would be the harm—wait. *My rig,* he'd said. He was a trucker? Would he give her a ride? Was she brave enough to try?

Could she make herself do that? Leave with a total stranger?

No. Absolutely not. But she had to find Uncle Roland. Had to figure out a way to get—

Where? Where did she go from here? What did she do? She wanted to lie down and sleep until all this was over.

"Never mind." He turned to go.

"Wait—" she said. "Yes, please. Join me."

He frowned.

"Sit down, Case," Jolene ordered, and at last he complied. She went on as though nothing had happened. "So what'll you have besides coffee, hot stuff? Some of that coconut cream pie you love?"

He took a minute and studied Samantha. "Pie sounds good. And bring her something filling and put it on my tab."

Before she could argue, Jolene spoke, beaming. "I've always said you're a nice man."

"Aw, Jolene, no call to insult me."

"Say what you want. I know what I know. I'll just go turn in her order and get your pie."

"No!"

They both looked oddly at her frantic tone.

"I mean, it hasn't been that long since I ate." If convenience store crackers and juice sometime yesterday counted.

"You sure?" he asked. His expression lost all teasing. His eyes held both doubt and compassion. A kindness that made her want to weep. "Then bring us two forks, Jolene."

"Sure thing. Back in a jiff." She departed.

He settled back in the booth and seemed to swallow up all the space and the air with it. "You can still say no. Jolene has a heart of gold, but she can be kinda like a nosy mom who loves you but won't stay out of your business." Fondness rang in his tone. "I'm Case Marshall, by the way." He extended a hand.

"Sama—Sammie," she stammered, and put her hand in his.

Big hand. Long, lean fingers. His warm hand cradled hers gently.

She shivered.

"You got a last name, Sammie? From Louisiana, right?"

She tensed. "How could you tell?"

"I can hear it in your voice…ah, Nawlins. One of my favorite places on earth."

Abruptly tears pricked at her eyes. Home had never seemed further away.

"You all right?"

She'd felt so alone. His kindness and Jolene's only made the sense of isolation worse.

"Fine." She straightened and said in a crisp imitation of her always-dignified mother. "Perfectly fine. And no, I'm not from New Orleans. I'm from…Lafayette."

She was lying. Case had traveled too much and dealt with too many people not to have a strongly-developed ability to read body language.

She was also scared to death of something. And way beyond tired.

But man, she was a beauty, those witchy blue eyes topped by delicately-arched eyebrows. Long, dark brown hair glowed red-gold like a bottle of Jack Daniels with sunlight pouring through it. The mass of curls made his fingers itch to dive right in, made him picture how it would feel to bury his face in them while he buried himself—

And he was staring.

While she was ready to bolt.

"Here you go," Jolene said, setting down his coffee and the pie with two forks.

Case sat up straight. "Thanks, Jolene."

"You sure you won't have a real meal?" she asked the woman.

"No, thank you."

Case forked up a bite, but when she didn't pick up her own utensil, he turned his fork to her. "You have to try this. It's pure heaven."

She hesitated...then her mouth opened and her tongue licked over the tines. Her eyes lowered as she savored the taste, her lips lingering, slightly parted, as the fork slid across them.

Holy—Case closed his eyes as his body reacted.

"Mmm..."

He stilled, his fork extended. His eyes followed the undulations of her throat as she swallowed, pleasure blossoming on her face.

He'd never look at coconut cream pie the same after this.

Jolene walked by. "Something wrong with the pie that you're not eating?"

Case's brain scrambled. "Uh...no. Fine—it's fine."

Jolene looked at him funny. "I'll check back."

"Thanks." He busied himself cutting his own bite.

Though he'd really rather watch her savor another one.

The woman whose name might or might not be Sammie finally took up her own fork but only twisted it in her fingers.

Even in the midst of a noisy room, the silence between them thundered.

"Do you—?"

"Where are you—?"

Their voices chimed in unison, and they halted, awkwardness filling the space between them.

"You first," he said.

"Do you come here often? It's…unusual, isn't it?"

Case grinned. "The owner intended this to resemble a medieval castle." He glanced around at what he'd long ago quit noticing. Stone and cedar mingled in the interior while outside the place had actual turrets. Roadside diner furnishings sat beneath water-stained, nicotine-browned acoustic ceiling tiles. In the convenience store at the entrance, they sold everything from a complete tool set to tiny ceramic poodles.

"It's in a class by itself." She smiled faintly, but her eyes were shadowed. Jolene was right—she looked thin and weary.

"Sure you don't want something more to eat? My treat?"

"No, thank you. I'm really not—" Her eyes misted. She looked away, battling for composure.

Case watched her struggle with her emotions, unsure what to do. He didn't have much practice at soothing—shoot, he'd practically invented the term *love 'em and leave 'em*. He'd been with his share of women in the past, but only the ones who were out for a good time. No way was Case Marshall getting within a mile of a woman who'd reach for his heart.

But this woman's eyes were filled with fear. Exhaustion he could understand, aggravation, too, even worry. But what kindled most strongly in Sammie's eyes was terror—why?

Don't you have enough problems to deal with, fleabrain? Why do you want to know about one more? You're supposed to be well on your way to the ranch by now. Eat up and get going.

"Is there anything I can help you with?" he found himself asking, anyway.

She studied him, those blue eyes sad and haunted. "I…" Then she closed them and shook her head.

"What? Tell me. I'll help if I can, but I can't read your mind."

Her gaze flew to his, and for a moment he saw hope spark. Then she glanced away. "You said you're in a hurry."

"What do you need?" *What kind of trouble are you in?* He hoped she didn't say money—he had little to spare. The ranch sucked up every last dime he could make.

She nibbled on that lush lower lip, and he had to tear his gaze away. "My car is a mile back down the road. Could you help me get it started?"

"Is that all?"

"I don't know what's wrong with it, and I don't want to delay you."

"Honey, the engine hasn't been made that I can't fix." He pointed out the window. "See that rig with the red cab right there? That's mine. You head that way, and I'll go pay our tab."

"Oh, you don't have to—"

"Didn't you hear Jolene say I'm a nice guy?"

She smiled for the first time. "You called that an insult."

"Well, yeah. Add that to harmless, and a guy could get a complex." He grinned at her. "Go on, now, and I'll be right out. We'll get you fixed up in no time."

"I don't know how to thank you."

"Don't call me harmless, and we'll be square."

Then she really smiled, and Case was doubly glad she would be gone soon.

Or he could be in real trouble.

Chapter Two

C ase stood waiting for his change from the cashier.
A scream split the air.

He looked around quickly, trying to spot Sammie.

When he did, he couldn't believe his eyes. Instead of being near his truck, she was struggling in the grasp of a man in a dark suit. Definitely not a fellow trucker, not duded up like that.

Weariness vaporized. He abandoned his change and ran for the door.

A second man jumped out of the driver's side of a nondescript sedan, leaving it standing wide open.

Outside Case spotted a short piece of lumber lying by the side of the building and paused to grab it. As he rounded the pump islands, he saw her manage to loosen one of her arms and drive her elbow right under her assailant's ribcage. The man, not as tall as Case but solid, cursed loudly as he struggled to keep one hand over her mouth and her arms pinned with his other arm.

His companion laughed, calling out to the stocky man. "Whatsa matter, Ray? You cain't handle one skinny woman, you?"

Cajun accent. Who were they? Why were they here?

The one called Ray turned thunderous at the insult. He used his huge paw to slap her so hard her head recoiled from the force of the blow.

A murderous rage swept through Case.

He charged the man with a roar.

Sammie went weak with relief when she heard Case shout. The men were from Gascoigne, she could tell from their first words, and she was terrified that they'd caught up to her so fast.

Her relief was short-lived.

The other thug grabbed her from behind and hauled her toward the car. He squeezed her midriff so hard, air burst from her lungs. She fought against his hold even as dark spots danced before her eyes.

He dragged her to the open car door while she gasped for air, and fear overcame weakness. She couldn't let him trap her inside. With one last effort, she launched herself to one side, and he lost his balance, hitting the sharp door edge hard.

A grunt of pain, but he never let go.

Then he swung one massive fist and cuffed the side of her head. "You do dat again, *chère*, and you won't like the way Frenchy makes you pay later."

Sammie's desperation rocketed. She'd been terrorized by Gascoigne's men once before, and she would never forget the stark understanding of her vulnerability.

To make his point, he ran thick fingers up her right thigh, then jerked her legs apart and shoved his meaty hand between them to cup her.

Revulsion gagged her. She renewed her fight, but his hand only tightened on her most private place. A whimper rose in her throat, and it was all she could do not to panic.

"Get your hands off her!" Case yelled. With a mighty swing of the wood in his hand, Case knocked the one called

Ray to the ground, stunning him with a fierce blow to the head. He charged toward her, vaulting over the hood of the car.

Frenchy picked her up and threw her into the back seat of the car so hard she slid across the vinyl and slammed into the passenger door. Pain exploded in her head.

Case was shouting her name, but she was too stunned to make out the words.

He roared again. "Sammie, get up! Get out of the car!"

But she couldn't move. Nausea swamped her.

"Sammie, *now!*" The car shuddered as Case slammed Frenchy against the rear panel.

Sammie struggled to right herself. She reached for the door handle, but her fingers wouldn't grip.

The door opened, and she nearly fell out. Jolene stepped forward and steadied her, lending support when her legs wobbled.

"Case—he's—" Sammie tried to find him.

Jolene's tone was gentle. "Sugar, friends are helping him now, don't you worry. You just stay here with me."

Her gaze at last settled on him.

Helping was not exactly the word she would have used. Two men restrained Frenchy, and one more knelt on Ray's back. Two others tried to keep Case from killing Frenchy.

Case cursed loudly and fought both of them. He landed a blow to the gut of one of the men, and two more rushed forward as he started after Frenchy again.

"Maybe we'd better let him see you. It might calm him down." Jolene drew her around the car toward Case.

"Case?" Sammie ventured. "Case, I'm okay."

He stilled and looked up. His eyes narrowed at the sight of her.

She took a step toward him—

And folded like a rag doll.

Jolene caught her as she fell.

Case abandoned the others and drew her from Jolene's grip.

"I'll call the sheriff," Jolene offered.

"No!" Sammie started to struggle. "Case, no—please—"

He frowned. "They can't get away with this," he said to her. "They need to be locked up."

"No—please, you can't—" She clasped his forearm. "I'm begging you."

Her terror was all too real.

And it had nothing to do with a broken-down car.

Blowing out a breath, he turned to Jolene. "Think you all can detain them so that I can get her out of here? I don't want them to see what I'm driving or our direction."

Jolene, experienced at dealing with rowdy customers without benefit of official help, nodded. "You know you can count on me, but don't you think you two had better see a doc first?"

Panic swept Sammie's features. "No! Please, can we just leave?"

What the hell was going on? He made a swift decision. "Give me some ice for her face, and we'll be on our way."

One of the other waitresses left to fetch some ice. She brought it back, wrapped in a plastic bag with a dishtowel around it.

"Thanks for your help," he said to those crowded around. "If you can keep this under your hats, I'd sure appreciate it. Too many people talking about this is going to make it easier for them to track her." He paused. "I don't like this. They should be made to pay."

The woman in his arms went rigid. Dug in her nails. "Just let me go and leave this alone, then. Please."

"Hell if I will."

"You two go on," Jolene said. "This is a tight-knit bunch. We'll keep a lid on it. Gonna be awhile before these two stir, anyway, I'm thinking."

But he still wanted to kick their asses for abusing this fragile woman.

Who owed him some answers.

"Thanks, Jolene." Sweeping Sammie up in his arms, he carried her to the truck, favoring his injured right knee. He lifted her gently into the passenger side of the cab, tucking her seat belt around her and arranging the ice pack against her cheek.

In the driver's seat, he glanced back to see the small crowd huddled around the two thugs lying facedown on the ground. His teeth ground. His adrenaline was still riding high, and he itched to finish the job he'd started.

He looked again at Sammie. Their gazes held in the dim light from the dashboard. Emotion, unnamed but no less powerful, surged between them, making the space suddenly close and intimate. The bloodlust roiling through Case was suddenly replaced by a rush of desire.

Sammie's eyes darkened.

Neither stirred for the space of a very long heartbeat.

The draw between them crackled.

Then she swayed, and he remembered himself. He cranked his engine. She was hurt, damn it. So was he.

"You're bleeding," she said.

Case put his hand to his cheek and felt the blood there. "I've had worse."

As he turned to away to drive, his knee throbbed like a sonofabitch, and he bit back a groan.

Sammie placed a hand on his arm. "Shouldn't you get someone to look at that knee? Just let me leave and you can—"

"No." What in hell was he thinking? He didn't need this, any of it. "If anyone's going to see a doctor, it's you."

"I'm okay."

"You're not okay. Are you dizzy?"

"Just…tired. I'll be fine."

Sure you will. She looked so damn sad. So scared.

Rage surged again, and he smacked the steering wheel. "What the hell was that? Who are those guys?"

Her shoulders curled inward. "I'm not sure."

"Then why let them go? And why would they want to kidnap you?"

She shrank into herself. "You don't have to get involved. Look, I'm grateful, but—" Defeat rode her features hard.

Chill out. She's hurt. He faced forward and pulled out of the lot. "Listen, I know I said I'd help you get your car running, but I can't say how long it might take, and I don't think stopping so close to here is the best idea, under the circumstances. Is there anyone you can call to take you back to it, once we get further down the road?"

"I'm sorry. You can just drop me off…" Her eyes filled.

"Do you even know where you're going? Come on, Sammie—tell me what you're running from."

"Could I—" She worried at her lower lip. "May I just rest for a minute? Please?"

She looked like a whipped pup. Even though he had a million questions, he didn't have the heart to push her any harder as she curled against the door.

He exhaled. "A little while, yeah." He had a good six hours before he got home. He could spare one or two, though what the hell he'd do with her—

"Thank you."

Those big blue eyes were the saddest thing he'd ever seen. Jesus.

"Get some sleep," he said gruffly. "Then we are having ourselves a chat."

For now he focused on getting them out of their safely.

They drove on through the emerging dawn.

"Where are we?" When she awoke, Sammie's voice was still muzzy, but she sounded a little less vague. She stretched like a cat, all lithe and sensual, her hair a whiskey tumble down her back. "And where are we going?"

He yanked his gaze away and focused on the road. "We're on I-20 headed west from Abilene. But I'm asking the questions now."

Out of the corner of his eye, he saw her tense.

"*First*, you tell me your real name." Bad enough he had a ranch barely hanging on by its fingernails and a crooked ex-partner who'd stolen him blind. He didn't have the luxury of playing Sir Galahad. Every mile that had passed, he'd berated himself for a fool. What did he think he was, some white knight? If he had a lick of sense, he'd just let her go.

She didn't answer right away as she stared straight ahead, an obvious struggle going on behind that beautiful facade.

He'd never bullied a woman, and he didn't want to start now. But something was more than a little out-of-whack here, and now he had a personal stake in it, like it or not. Just as he was about to press her again, she spoke.

"St. Claire." Barely a whisper.

"What?"

"St. Claire. That's my last name. And Sammie is short for Samantha."

Okay. Better.

"*Now* will you tell me where we're going?" she snapped.

He nearly grinned. Sassy was better than terrified. "My ranch."

"You have a ranch? Where is it?"

"Near Post, not far from Lubbock. Do you know where that is?"

She shook her head. "Sorry, I'm afraid I've never been

west of Houston until now."

"I have a cousin who used to be a detective in Houston. His ranch isn't that far from mine—at least in Texas terms."

"So, what, only two or three hundred miles?"

Yep, definitely sassy. He did grin, after all. "Practically next door." He paused. Time to dig some more. "You're not from Lafayette, are you?"

She was silent for a long moment, then she shook her head. "New Orleans."

"I lived there once."

"Where?"

"Nowhere you'd ever want to go." He shrugged. "It was long time back."

"You must have been pretty young, then."

I'm not sure I was ever young. "I left home at sixteen, so I'd been on the road a long time. I felt older."

Her hand brushed his arm lightly. "I'm sorry."

He shrugged. "Water under the bridge."

"Didn't your parents miss you?" She halted, her breeding evident. "I'm sorry—I shouldn't have asked."

"My dad sure as hell didn't. My mother was dead."

"I'm so sorry."

"Don't be." He gentled his voice. "She'd already been gone for several years. As for my old man, I'm sure he was glad to see me go." Weird feeling, discussing this. He'd never talked to anyone about leaving home, not even Wiley. The lady was no doubt shocked.

"But—" she started.

"But what? People don't hate their kids in your safe little world?" No matter what he'd tried, he'd never been able to please Jack Marshall. Case had long ago accepted his failure to be someone worthy of his father's love.

He shook off old memories. "Enough of that. What's going on? You're clearly on the run—from what? And who were those guys?"

For a moment, he didn't think she was going to answer.

"I think they might have been sent by the man I was seeing. He didn't want to take no for an answer."

"Then why not get the cops involved? Get a restraining order?"

"He's…a powerful man. It's not that easy."

Anger simmered. "Did he hurt you?"

Her shoulders curved inward. "Yes," she barely whispered.

His hands clenched on the wheel. The urge to turn back and give the guy some of his own medicine was powerful.

But he had a ranch waiting. People who depended on him.

"Come with me," he said.

"What?" She looked over.

"Come to my ranch. You'll be safe."

After a long moment, she responded. "Seriously?" Her voice mingled disbelief and…hope. "Oh, I couldn't ask you to—"

"You didn't," he interrupted. "I offered. I mean, it's not much, but it's isolated and way off the beaten path."

What the hell was he doing? *You have lost your mind for sure, son.* "Look, if you don't want to, no big deal. I just can't fool around because I'm needed there and—"

"Yes."

His head whipped around. "Yes?"

Her lips were pressed together, her eyes glistening. She looked so damn fragile. "Thank you. Oh, thank you, Case. I promise I won't be any trouble, and I won't stay long, just until—" One tear fell. "I'll get this figured out, I promise."

Well, he was in the soup now. Too late to back out, not when a beautiful, wounded woman was looking at him like he was some kind of hero.

He almost snorted. She'd find out soon enough. He was no hero.

The next couple of miles passed in silence. He wondered if she was having second thoughts, too.

At last she spoke. "What does it look like? Where your ranch is, I mean."

"It's harsh country, open and vast. You can see miles in every direction, and it reminds you that you're only a man, that the land will always be the victor, that you're lucky if she lets you eke out a living."

"Are we close yet?" she asked.

"Another hour before we stop for fuel. I'm going to call a friend near Snyder who'll let me park the truck on his deer lease. It's covered with mesquites, so the truck won't be easy to spot there. I'll get my foreman, Wiley, to meet us there and take us on to the ranch. In case our friends back there got a look at my truck when we left, I want us to be seen headed west on I-20 so maybe whoever's following you will keep heading that way."

"You've done so much for me." She sank against the door. She looked beat.

"How does your head feel now? Still dizzy?"

"It hurts some, but there's only one of you looking at me now."

"I guess one's enough, huh?"

She smiled. "I'm betting women like looking at you."

That smile was a killer.

Ditto, babe. He cleared his throat. "You can climb in the sleeper to nap until we have to stop for fuel."

"I'm fine here." She touched his arm. "Case, I don't know how to thank you. I'm so sorry I got you mixed up in this. If you want to drop me off at the next stop, I'll understand."

Their gazes held for a long beat, then Case turned back to the road, jaw working. There were many things he wanted to do with her. Leaving her wasn't one of them.

"You go ahead and sleep now."

Maybe while she did, he'd recover what little good sense he had left.

Chapter Three

The darkness inside her apartment felt different. Felt…wrong.

A faint scrape against the wall to her left. The hairs on her neck stood on end. Fear prickled down her spine. She turned toward the noise, her back against the wall of her foyer.

Anticipation. The animal sense of being stalked. She felt someone close.

No one she knew would play a game like this.

Her phone was at the bottom of her purse. No way she could reach it without making sound.

Go back or go forward? She'd already thrown the dead-bolt on her door.

Suddenly a large frame loomed.

She couldn't help the quick gasp.

A big hand clad in latex clamped over her mouth. The man spun her around, shoving her face into the wall. Pressed his hulking frame against her backside, mashing her breasts painfully against the unyielding surface. She shuddered in horror as she felt his erection pressing against the curve of her behind, only the thin silk of her dress separating her from him.

The sour smell of his sweat rolled over her. She struggled to breathe, her mind recoiling in horror as she struggled against him, every movement bringing his body in contact with hers…

Case heard Sammie panting in her sleep, her face contorted by fear, whimpering as she stirred restlessly.

"Sammie?" He touched her shoulder.

She screamed, her eyes popping wide with naked terror. She scrambled against the door, revulsion and horror sweeping over her features.

"Hey…it's okay…it's only me, Case."

Eyes glazed, she shrank back, frantically trying to get away.

"Sammie…Sammie, hold on." Case pulled over on the shoulder, glad the traffic was light in mid-morning out here.

He reached for her, and she fought him. "Please don't hurt me…please…"

"Sh-h, it's me, Case." He tried again, stroking her arm gently. "It's okay, honey. You're safe." He wrapped one arm around her and kept his voice soft. "Sh-h, it's okay, I promise. It's only a dream. You're safe," he repeated. As if she were a child, he stroked her hair slowly.

Slowly she subsided, still trembling in his arms. With careful, steady movements, he lifted her onto his lap and cradled her tenderly, wrapping her securely within his embrace. He laid his cheek on top of her head and rocked her gently. Tears streamed down her face, and she burrowed closer.

It was a new feeling for Case, this tenderness, this wish to shield a woman, to protect her from harm. There was so much he didn't understand about her, so many reasons of his own to stay away, but he didn't know how he could turn his back on her, however much he didn't need the complications of her presence—to say nothing of the man who would send two bruisers after her.

What the hell he'd do with her, though, he had no idea.

So he simply held on and let her cry.

At last the tears slowed. She tilted her head back to look at him. Stared at his mouth, her pupils going wide and soft.

The atmosphere in the cab shifted.

The press of her body against his was a slow burn, desire a river of gold, sparking within him a yearning to forget what was sensible, to ignore reason…to taste her just for a moment, before he had to remember his responsibilities. He lowered his mouth to hers.

In the first instant he knew one kiss would never be enough. All the adrenaline of the past hours swept through him again, fueling within him a hunger that one kiss could not stem.

Bathed in longing, desperate for oblivion, Sammie opened to him, starved for the feast his dark beauty promised, hungering for the joining. She arched to him, her body urging his closer. His clever tongue swept within, his touch raising goosebumps on her skin, her blood thickening like dark honey.

A passing truck sounded its air horn.

They both jolted.

Their gazes locked for one long, charged moment.

Then, though reality was creeping in too fast, he lingered to place a lush, wet kiss on the sensitive pulse point in her neck. He caressed the side of her breast, trailing his fingers up to cradle her cheek, then traced her lips with one long finger, rubbing them softly…slowly…

Suspended in silent wonder, Sammie knew she should straighten and move to her seat, but she wanted only to open herself to him, to arch against him once more, to spiral downward into his dark spell.

Case's voice was husky when he spoke. "This isn't over." With one last, mesmerizing gesture, he caressed her full lower lip with his thumb and lowered his head.

He swirled that dangerous, promising tongue one last time over the contours of her mouth, and she moaned.

When he picked her up and set her back in her own seat, Sammie grasped for a foothold in a world that had shifted.

Case rolled the truck into place at the fuel pump. Since he'd set her back in her seat, he'd wrapped silence around him like armor. The stranger was back, all the tenderness and every speck of passion had vanished.

But Sammie couldn't forget the man who'd fought to save her. His actions spelled out a different man than his guarded silence. Few people would have gone out of their way for a perfect stranger to the extent Case had.

But where did they go from here?

Where did *she* go, she cautioned herself as she got down from the high perch while he fueled his truck. She couldn't let herself forget that she was alone in this—she, who once had a tightly-knit world at her beck and call. Oh, of course her Papa was overbearing, but there was no doubt that he loved her. He had created a life for his family that, while sometimes stifling, was supportive and all-encompassing, a gossamer womb in which they were all safely ensconced.

Look at her now, Samantha St. Claire, formerly the much-envied Queen of Rex at Mardi Gras. Would anyone in her social circle ever have imagined a day when she'd trade her jeweled ballgown for the life of a fugitive?

She couldn't afford to be this dependent on anyone. She'd already cost Case too much, and from the condition of his truck, he didn't have a lot of resources to spare.

Coming around the back of the truck, she stopped a minute to look at Case as he stood by the pump. Weariness and pain hovered in the lines of his body, but pride kept his back straight.

He was a handsome devil. His was the dark, compelling beauty of a Lucifer, a dark angel unafraid to test the boundaries—of desire, of passion, of the prescribed ways of behavior agreed upon by polite society. She had no difficulty imagining that Case had rebelled before and would do so again. Her circumspect existence in New Orleans would never have led her to cross paths with someone like him.

Despite all that had befallen her this night, she thought she was glad that she had.

"Is it very lonely on the road?" Sammie spoke up for the first time since they'd gotten back on the highway. The long silence was giving her too much time to think, with no answers in sight. She was desperate to forget her own problems.

"Sometimes. It's not for everyone. You have to like your own company a lot, or hate everyone else's enough to endure it. You can go for days with only a few minutes' conversation, if that's the way you want it. But sometimes, out there on the road, you can forget everything else for a while. Other times, too much time to think can drive you crazy."

She could certainly relate to that. Something in his tone made Sammie wonder what it was he wanted to forget.

Case Marshall was a real puzzle. It was easy to assume he had little education, given that he'd left home at sixteen, but his wits were sharp and his intelligence clear. He intrigued her, this strong and powerful man, capable of violent rage and great tenderness. He didn't shy from brute force, but she couldn't imagine him using it for dishonorable purposes. He'd defended her, cared for her…opened his home to her.

Sobering, she reminded herself that she knew next to nothing about him—and most of what he knew about her was lies. *Don't get too comfortable. You're in big trouble, and you haven't outrun it yet.*

Case saw the sudden frown that marred her lovely face and

assumed she must be thinking about the man she feared. He could ask her, but she seemed to be as tired as he was. It had been a tumultuous few hours since they'd met.

He settled back, wondering at the contradictions of this elusive woman, the many faces of her he'd seen. He thought of the wildcat; he remembered the lady. She might be patrician, but she was not a snob. She'd treated Jolene with courtesy and a gracious warmth, despite how nervous and frightened she'd been, and that surprised him.

Case had spent most of his life in the company of the common folk who made up the backbone of society. He'd also spent time with the roughest elements.

From the invisible position of the bartender or the valet parking attendant, he'd also logged numerous hours in the company of those considered society's finest. This woman was different. He could easily imagine her in a ballgown or seated behind a desk giving orders, but she treated someone like Jolene, whom most of them would never even notice, with a genuine friendliness that spoke volumes about her true nature.

One more time, Case wondered what in heaven's name he thought he was doing.

And how he'd explain his decision to bring her home to Wiley and Linnie Mae, when he couldn't even explain it to himself.

The windmill nearby creaked as it turned, the tank at its base brimming with dark water, deep green with algae, flashes of gold from the huge goldfish swimming in the small space. As the wind picked up, the windmill whirred, and the laboring creak increased its frequency.

Sammie stood under a shade tree, fanning herself with a

piece of paper she'd found in the truck. She held her hair up off her neck and closed her eyes with a sigh of pleasure.

Case wouldn't let himself look over at the sound of her sigh. It wasn't a far cry from the sounds she'd made as he'd caressed her. If Wiley wasn't due here any minute…

Shaking his head to ward off the direction his thoughts were straying, he turned away to watch for Wiley's arrival. He'd hidden the truck carefully, and he was ready to get home.

Just then he spotted a cloud of dust in the distance. He squinted in the sunlight and recognized Wiley's old brown Ford lumbering their way. He smiled, thinking about Wiley's harrumphing and snorting on the phone. That old man had a heart of purest gold which he felt duty-bound to hide behind a crotchety exterior that fooled no one. Right now, Case couldn't think of anyone he'd rather see, cranky or not.

Maybe Wiley could knock some sense into him.

The old man pulled to a stop near them and emerged from the truck, his legs bowed from years and years on horseback. He had a jaunty walk, exaggerated by his scuffed boots with their old-style heels and pointy toes. Wiley scoffed at the idea of wearing anything else, a horseman through and through. His weathered face framed bright blue eyes with laugh lines etched deep around them. For all his efforts at playing the curmudgeon, Wiley was one of the most relentlessly cheerful people Case had ever known.

Case turned and beckoned to Sammie. When she neared, Wiley removed his hat, showing a shock of pure white hair.

Wiley's eyes widened as he took in Sammie's beauty. Case could tell that his appreciation nearly displaced the frank curiosity. Gentleman to the end, however, he merely said, "Ma'am" and nodded. He'd often told Case that his mama would have whipped him for not taking off his hat to a lady.

"This is Sammie St. Claire, Wiley. She's going to be coming back to the ranch with us." Case didn't want to make her self-conscious, so he didn't even try to explain why.

Wiley took it in stride. "Well, Miss St. Claire, I never saw Case bring home anything as pretty as you before. The boy might amount to something yet."

Case snorted.

Sammie smiled and held out her hand. "Please call me Sammie, Mr. Cantrell. I'm not sure Case is bringing home such a bargain. I'm a little worse for wear." She glanced down ruefully at her wrinkled clothes.

"I'll be glad to call you Sammie if you'll call me Wiley." He placed his left hand over their clasped ones, patting hers. "And you look just fine to me, but let's get you home and let you clean up."

She looked so lonely then. So fragile Case wanted to sweep her up again. Make foolish promises.

He settled for a gentle touch to her arm. "Ready?"

She nodded and squared her shoulders. "I am." She smiled at Wiley. "Thank you for coming to pick us up, Mr. Cantrell."

"Wiley," he reminded her. "You just come on now, little lady, and we'll fix you right up."

Apparently Case wasn't the only white-knight fool in the bunch.

Chapter Four

"Sammie, we're here." Case's voice urged her up from her dreamworld.

She sat up, realizing that she had fallen asleep on his shoulder. Wiley and Case had been talking about happenings on the ranch, naming people she couldn't keep straight. She had been grateful they didn't ask her any questions, and soon the motion of the old pickup had lulled her to sleep, tucked between the two of them.

She rolled her head to work out the kinks in her neck and saw Case moving his shoulder, too. She winced. "Sorry, I didn't mean to fall asleep. You shouldn't have let me hurt your shoulder."

"It's not hurt, just stiff. And you needed the rest."

"You probably do, too. When's the last time you slept?"

"I'll sleep later." His tone brooked no argument.

She saw Wiley's eyes crinkle at the corners as if he wanted to laugh. He pointed to both sides of the road and gestured to the bluffs in the distance. "This here is the Flying M, Sammie." Pride filled his voice, his love for the land obvious.

Sammie took in the vista before her, harsh yet strangely beautiful. Mesquites dotted the landscape. The bluffs in the distance were striated with bands of cream, gold, and terra cotta. The red dirt glowed in the sunlight.

Ahead to the right was a large clump of trees, and she

could make out the outlines of several barns and outbuildings. The air seemed cleaner, somehow, and even in the heat of midday, there was a crispness which she found invigorating.

She had this sense of…possibility. For the first time she understood why the pioneers kept pushing west, away from the crowded cities.

She noticed Case watching her and smiled. "It's beautiful."

He looked surprised. Maybe gratified. "You think so?" He looked around, too, as if he were seeing it anew.

The white frame house came into view. "Oh, Case, it's lovely." Two stories high, the entire house was encircled by a wide porch. Though Sammie saw nothing like the formal landscaping or lush greenery she would see in New Orleans, the house was perfectly in tune with its setting. Near the front door, a porch swing hung. On the other side sat two wooden chairs with thick cushions. The porch itself was so deep that the inside of the house would probably stay cool even in the heat of summer. Big windows stood open, letting the cooling wind blow through.

The trees were few in number, but a large one shaded the west side of the house from the harsh sun, and lacy mesquites spread out in all directions. A windmill churned behind the house, and beyond that she spotted corrals.

As they rolled to a stop in front of the house, two small children came running around from the side. A tiny older woman with an apron over her jeans opened the front door. She stepped out onto the porch, shading her eyes as she walked down the steps. When she saw Case, she opened her arms for a hug. Sammie couldn't repress a smile at the sight of the tall Case almost bent over double hugging the woman whose arms barely reached around his back. They lingered there, her talking a mile a minute in his ear.

"Linnie Mae's always felt like Case was her boy, especially since his own mama died when he was young," Wiley observed. "She fusses over him like a mama hen, and he puts up with her meddling pretty well. He knows there's nothing she wouldn't do for him."

Sammie tried not to be nervous when Case walked over to her with his arm around the small woman's shoulders. "Linnie Mae, I'd like you to meet Sammie St. Claire."

Linnie Mae's light gray eyes avidly searched Sammie's face, but she smiled, saying, "Welcome to the Flying M, Sammie. We're glad to have you here."

"Thank you very much, Mrs. Cantrell. I appreciate your hospitality."

"Case! Case!" Two wriggling children competed for his attention, a boy of about three or four and a girl a year or two older—Sammie wasn't sure. She hadn't spent much time around kids. Her younger sisters were both married, but neither had children yet.

The boy's arm wrapped around Case's right leg as he stood wedged between Case and Linnie Mae. He looked up at her shyly out of soft brown eyes, solemnly watching with the thumb of his other hand in his mouth. His sister pulled at Case's left hand, begging for his attention.

"Case, Case, who's the pretty lady? How come her clothes are all dirty?"

Sammie brushed at her skirt, mortified to have forgotten how she must look.

"Jennifer, mind your manners," Linnie Mae scolded.

The little girl's face fell.

Case glanced at Sammie as if asking what explanation she wanted.

Sammie spoke up. "I, um, had a little accident. I don't have a change of clothes because my car wouldn't start anymore, and I had to leave it behind. My suitcase was in there."

Case dropped into a crouch to look in the girl's eyes. "This pretty lady's name is Sammie, Jennifer, and we're going to help her out." He hoisted the boy onto his shoulders, then stood, reclaiming the little girl's hand.

"I'm sorry you got hurt," Jennifer said.

"Thank you. I'm very grateful that Case came to my rescue."

The children fastened their eyes on Case again. The boy's free hand patted Case's hair. His sister was obviously impressed. "Case, you're a hero! I'm gonna go to tell Ralph you saved the pretty lady." Whirling, she took off for the back of the house.

Her brother's legs pumped madly on Case's chest as he wriggled to get down and follow. Case lifted him off his shoulders and set him on the ground, removing the boy's thumb before he patted him on the rear and let him go. "You'd better hustle if you're gonna catch up."

David took off at a run, chubby legs pumping. "Jennifer, *wait*, Jennifer, wait for me-ee," his mournful howl sounded.

"Those two…" Wiley shook his head with a fond grin. "In case you couldn't tell, they're our grandchildren," he explained.

"What am I thinking of?" Linnie Mae said. "You both must be exhausted. I waited dinner for you." She grasped Sammie's arm. "Come on in out of the heat before you burn that pretty skin of yours." She didn't wait for Case and Wiley to follow.

"Another chick to brood over." Wiley laughed and slapped Case on the back. "Come on in, or I'll eat your share."

Case chuckled and followed him inside.

The meal was a noisy, happy time. Sammie learned that in ranch country, they called the noon meal dinner and the evening meal was called supper; lunch was a city word. The size of the meal surprised her, but she reasoned that the people eating it were doing hard physical labor and needed more fuel than someone sitting at a desk all day. She tried to keep the names straight as she looked around the big oval table.

Linnie Mae seated her next to Case. Jennifer promptly claimed the spot next to Sammie. David sat beside his sister, perched on a little box to raise him up to table height. On his other side sat his grandfather. Linnie Mae was beside Wiley, and the only permanent ranch hand, Ralph Parker, completed the table. From time to time, Sammie saw him cast admiring glances her way, blushing every time she caught him. Given her current state of disarray, she couldn't imagine why.

"Hey, Case, guess what Ralph did this morning?" Wiley's grin spoke of pure mischief.

"Don't tell me you decided to try Comanche again?"

"Hell, no, Case, I ain't that stupid. Nobody around here wants to tangle with that mean sumbitch horse of yours."

"Ralph Parker, watch your mouth. There's a lady present," Linnie Mae remonstrated.

"Sorry, Miss St. Claire, didn't mean nothin' by it," Ralph mumbled, his ears burning bright red.

"Please call me Sammie, Ralph. No offense taken."

She found herself relaxing, listening to the good-natured ribbing as Wiley sketched out an encounter between Ralph and a bull, and Case teased the young man. Everything felt so...normal. The cozy atmosphere of this enchanted circle lifted her spirits.

Her problems were far from gone. She still had to find a way out of her nightmare, but in this moment, she would enjoy the respite. Remember how it felt to be a normal person with an everyday life.

A sly remark from Wiley made her burst out laughing. She saw Case look at her, a tender grin on his face. She didn't look away, and the spark of laughter in his green eyes burned down to a dark, glowing ember. She barely breathed, a slow thrill sizzling through her.

The sudden stillness around the table never registered.

Fortunately for Case and Sammie, David had had enough of good behavior. He wiggled and clamored to get down. The group scattered as the workload beckoned, leaving Wiley at the back door, while Case, Sammie and Linnie Mae stood around the table. Sammie began to pick up dishes to help with the cleanup.

Linnie Mae would hear none of it. "Shoo now, child. Let me show you to your room. You look like you need to rest. And I might have something you could wear."

Sammie was tired, but she wasn't ready to leave the cozy kitchen or the warm gathering.

Case took the decision out of her hands when he grabbed the plates she held and carried them to the counter. "She's right, Sammie, you do need to rest. I want to be sure you recover fully from the blow to your head."

"What?" Wiley and Linnie Mae exclaimed in unison.

"It's really nothing. I'm feeling fine now."

"Nonsense, young lady, come here and let me look at you. Did she lose consciousness, Case?"

"No, and I kept an eye on her. But she was pretty dizzy for a while."

"Come on upstairs with me. Let's take a look at you," Linnie Mae hustled her out of the room.

Sammie frowned over her shoulder at Case, who only grinned and shrugged helplessly. "Case is limping, if you didn't notice. He hurt his knee."

His grin turned to a scowl. "I'm fine. See to her."

"I'll be looking you over, too, young man, once I get her settled," Linnie Mae warned him.

Sammie smirked at him but allowed Linnie Mae to lead her up the stairs without further protest. Once they were out of hearing, however, she made another pitch. "Case has had less sleep than I have. He's been through a lot for me in the last several hours."

"I can see how tired he is, but he won't sleep until he's looked things over with Wiley. I'll keep an eye on him and get him off that knee as soon as I can."

Linnie Mae drew her into a bedroom at the back of the house, then showed her the bathroom and where the towels were. "Will you be all right by yourself? Are you still dizzy?"

"No, I'm only tired, but a bath sounds like heaven. Thank you." Once the door was closed, Sammie removed the clothes she'd been in for over twenty-four hours, wishing she could burn them.

She washed her hair with the only shampoo she could see, a no-nonsense bargain brand. Jean-Claude would have a coronary if he knew that the locks he so carefully maintained were being abused this way. Sammie couldn't stem a smile.

Surprisingly, her hair felt as clean as it ever had with Jean-Claude's expensive concoctions. She'd never tried anything ordinary—her mother was all about a proper grooming routine with every beauty aid known to man, and she'd raised her daughters that way.

Linnie Mae obviously saw no need for pampering her short cap of silver hair. Her down-to-earth attitude made Sammie wonder about Linnie Mae as a mother.

She'd probably been wonderful. A real hands-on mother, unlike her own. Sammie had been raised by a succession of nannies, her father's idea of proper upbringing.

A knock sounded at the door. "Sammie? You all right in there?"

"Yes, ma'am. I'm just about perfect."

Linnie Mae chuckled. "Nothing like getting clean, is there? I'm just going to hang this shift on the door handle for whenever you're finished. It will probably be short on you, but it ought to work."

"Thank you." She didn't think these people had much in

the way of material wealth, yet their generosity had not abated.

A few minutes later, her hair drying in damp waves, the plain cotton shift stopping well short of her knees, Sammie emerged. She'd rinsed out her red silk lingerie and hung it over the shower rod. She felt a little self-conscious about leaving it there, but she didn't know what else to do. No telling when she'd be able to get replacements.

The bedroom was cheery, its wooden floors dotted with scattered throw rugs. A lovely quilt covered the bed, and a fan circled lazily overhead. On the closet door, Linnie Mae had hung a long red cotton skirt and a white peasant blouse, both clearly too large for the tiny woman.

"These belonged to our daughter," Linnie Mae explained. "She and her husband passed away a year ago in an automobile accident. That's why the little ones are with us."

"Oh, Mrs. Cantrell, I couldn't—"

"Nonsense, child. It's silly to waste them. I'm sorry it's all I have to offer, but I gave the rest away. Lucinda loved this outfit, so I—" She turned away.

She couldn't wear something so precious. "Mrs. Cantrell…"

"Linnie Mae, please, Sammie." With a discreet wipe of her eyes, the little woman straightened. "It would please me if you'd wear them, unless they're not—that is, these are not fancy clothes like the ones you were wearing."

"Oh no, that's not it. I just—what if I spilled something on them, or…" She left off helplessly. "They're your memories, Linnie Mae."

Linnie Mae grasped her hands tightly. "Honey, I have a heart full of memories, and I only have to look at Jennifer to see my Lucinda every day. Please, it would make me happy to do this. And don't worry if you spill something on them. I'm only sorry I don't have more."

Sammie hugged the woman. "Thank you."

With a sniff, Linnie Mae returned to business. "Now sit

down here, and let me look you over and make sure you're all right."

Sammie put herself in Linnie Mae's capable hands, sitting quietly on the bed while Linnie Mae examined her, clucking her tongue and muttering to herself but refraining from asking questions. She went into the bathroom briefly for peroxide. When she returned, she never showed it if she was scandalized by Sammie's red lingerie. She simply tucked Sammie into the big, comfortable bed with a light cover, drew the shades down and left the room.

If she'd thought it would be difficult to sleep in a strange place, the drone of the cicadas outside combined with the warm feeling of being tucked in by Linnie Mae to lull her to sleep almost before her head touched the pillow.

Wiley gave Case a piercing look and raised one eyebrow.

Case sighed deeply, then removed his cap as he scratched his head, looking across the back yard. "It's a long story, Wiley."

"Seems to me we got some time here, Case."

"Yeah, well…let's walk over to the barn."

"Gonna tell me what happened to your leg?"

"It's part of the long story." He proceeded to outline the events of the night.

Wiley frowned as he listened but didn't interrupt.

"I don't know much about those men who tried to kidnap her, except there's a man she's afraid of, and he sent them. She says he's a powerful man and she doesn't dare involve the police. She has no one to turn to, so…" Case turned up his hands. "Next thing I knew I was asking her to come here. I can't tell you why. She's scared to death and she's had one hell of a night, so I'm letting it ride for now."

"Looks like you haven't had such a great night yourself, son." Wiley's brow wrinkled with concern. "You sure she's not on the lam from the law?"

"She sure doesn't seem like the criminal type."

"Naw, she's every inch a lady, even all beat up like that. But we got to know what we're dealing with here, Case. It's not like we don't have plenty of problems already."

Case exhaled in a gust. "I know that. I tried to walk away in the beginning. I've got plenty to handle without this, but I just couldn't see what else to do. She hasn't asked a thing of me, Wiley, and she's been grateful for what little I've done."

Wiley snorted. "It doesn't sound like *little* quite covers this. Not as though either of you got off lightly."

Case shrugged. "I'm okay. Tell me what's been happening and why you needed me back so fast."

"Got another notice from the bank. Next time, it'll be a foreclosure notice."

Case swore darkly, looking away. "Goddamn that Bracewell all to hell. Why didn't I see it coming in time to stop him?"

"You weren't the only one around here, Case. None of us saw it coming." Wiley took off his hat and scratched his head. "Drank a lot of cups of coffee with Roland Bracewell. Never thought anything was wrong with him except his taste in suits."

Case shook his head. He couldn't see the humor in Roland's white Southern planter suits anymore. "I gave him too much rope."

"You had your hands full, digging up new business for the trucking company and running the ranch. You drove a lot of extra loads, too, just to make things work. You can't be everywhere at once."

Case pinched the bridge of his nose. "I should have sensed it somehow. The buck stops here."

"There wouldn't be a *here* if it wasn't for you. Jack left this place hanging by a thread. You performed a miracle with that idea of yours, setting up a trucking operation. It let us haul our cattle for free. Nobody around here works harder than you. You're not God, Case—and best I know, you don't have a crystal ball."

Staring off into the distance, Case wondered. "I should never have taken on a partner."

"You didn't have a choice. It was the only way. You'd have made enough to buy him out, too, if he hadn't taken off with every thin dime. You'd made a heck of a start." Wiley's head shook from side to side. "I drank a few whiskeys with Roland, too. Never once did he let on that he wasn't what he seemed. I'd swear—I'd *still* swear that he wanted to make this work."

Case exploded. "Then why the hell did he take off and leave us holding the bag? Why make us lose every truck but that piece of junk I'm driving? Why push us to the brink of losing everything?"

He swore and picked up his pace, headed toward the barn. There was nothing to be gained by any more speculation about Roland Bracewell's intentions. "Let's get ready for auction, Wiley. One day at a time, that's all we can do. I'll find some extra runs to make, and I'll talk to the bank. See if they'll give us more time." Shoulders stiffened against the blow he could see coming, Case tried to blank out everything except the cattle he needed to select for auction.

Chapter Five

"*Imbécile*! How could you have let her escape?" Etienne Gascoigne's voice rose to a furious pitch.

"This situation should never have been allowed to get out of hand. How do you explain your inability to capture one small female, Frenchy?"

He sighed deeply as the voice on the phone blustered the reasons for their failure. He pinched the bridge of his nose and prayed for patience.

John Whitehead was a fool—first, for letting gambling become an obsession, second for allowing a pissant bookie like Roland Bracewell to become a blackmailer. Bracewell was a two-bit hustler, a small fry who was beneath Gascoigne's notice.

If banker Whitehead had controlled his desire to gamble, he would never have needed to resort to making fraudulent loans to come up with the sums he required to support his habit. That was not Gascoigne's concern, however. Whitehead was welcome to his habit; it kept him under their control. But he should have been smarter about covering his tracks.

"You know I will not tolerate failure. You find that woman and bring her back here, whatever it takes. Until we are certain of the extent of her knowledge, she must not be left on her own. Do you understand me, Frenchy? Whatever it takes, *comprends*?" He slammed down the receiver and began to pace.

Whitehead had been useful to them in the past; he could still be useful in the future, if this distasteful situation could be resolved favorably. As a Senior Vice President, he had the authority to place their various legitimate cash businesses on the bank's list of companies whose currency transactions need not be reported to the government. That greatly enhanced their ability to launder money. It would not be so easy to groom a replacement if Whitehead were rendered useless.

Gascoigne turned to the man who waited patiently for his orders. "What luck are you having tracing Bracewell?" He listened intently for moment, suppressing the urge to pound the desk.

Bracewell must also be found. He must turn over the evidence he had collected. He, of course, could not be allowed to live once he did. The niece was more problematical. Armand St. Claire's high visibility in the community created difficulties, as did his straight-arrow reputation. Gascoigne hoped the woman would continue to be neutralized with the threat of harm to her family—that had proven an effective ploy. Perhaps he had erred in sending his men after her; her fear alone might have caused her to stay away for a long time. He had to give Frenchy that much; the man's usual brutal tactics had certainly proven effective in terrifying her.

Gascoigne turned to his minion, pinning him with a menacing stare. His voice quietly intense, he spoke once more.

"Find Bracewell."

And Frenchy, you lovely bestial machine, find the woman.

Chapter Six

Sammie stretched, arching her back like a cat. A sense of well-being suffused her.

Then reality flooded back, and she remembered all she'd fled.

How trouble had already caught up with her once.

How she couldn't go home or she'd endanger her family.

Sound filtered in...cattle bawling, the voices of men. The whinny of horses.

She was really on a ranch. In some part of Texas she could barely identify. The breeze was cool in the early morning, and the scent of honeysuckle drifted through the screen.

She wrinkled her nose in delight. She always connected that scent with her maternal grandmother. At Nana's house, the bedroom in which she slept had its window shaded by a trellis bowed under the weight of thick, lush honeysuckle. In the spring and summer, she would awaken to its aroma. To this day, she connected the aroma with a feeling of safety, of being cherished.

She arose from the bed and walked to the window, then leaned on the windowsill. Sure enough, a fence was covered with honeysuckle close by. Activity off to her right drew her eye. She quickly spotted Case on horseback, recognizing him in spite of the straw cowboy hat that shielded his face. He wore leather work gloves, jeans, a khaki shirt and boots. He and the big roan moved as one, working the cattle, cutting this one and that out of the herd and guiding them to the two gooseneck trailers lined up near the corrals.

This, she realized, was his natural element. He might drive a truck, for whatever reason, but he belonged on this ranch.

As though he felt her scrutiny, Case suddenly looked up at her window, pausing to grin and tip his hat in her direction. His movement drew the attention of the others working with him, and they all turned to see what he had spotted. Sammie stepped back, aware that she wasn't presentable.

But oh, that smile…

Retrieving her lingerie from the bathroom, Sammie fervently hoped that the deep flounce around the neckline of the white blouse would serve to hide the vivid color of her bra. Going without went against every tenet with which she'd been raised, but her lingerie choices were even more limited than her wardrobe.

Just one more problem that couldn't be held at bay indefinitely.

As she neared the kitchen, she heard Linnie Mae humming. Once again, nostalgic memories suffused her. Her grandmother had hummed as she worked in the kitchen.

"Good morning, young lady." Linnie Mae was as cheerful today as yesterday. Looking Sammie over, she smiled. "They're lovely on you."

Sammie had the urge to apologize again for wearing her daughter's clothes. "Good morning, Linnie Mae. I'm sorry I slept all the way through."

"Oh, child, don't worry one little bit. You were all tuckered out. I'm glad you got some rest, but I'm sorry you missed supper. How about some coffee and a good breakfast? I've got biscuits and gravy I can warm up, and it won't take me two shakes to cook you some eggs and bacon."

"Coffee is plenty—and maybe one of those gorgeous biscuits, if you don't mind." She'd never seen any so fluffy.

"But, honey, you didn't have any supper."

She really was starving. "I'm not going to ask you to cook for me."

"It won't take two shakes. Here's a biscuit to tide you over, and coffee's over there."

"Is Case all right this morning?"

"That boy was ready to drop in his tracks last night. He should have taken a nap like you, but instead, he went out to help Wiley and the boys ready the stock for auction. I know he misses this place when he's on the road, even if he won't admit it. He always jumps right back in as soon as he returns, no matter how tired he might be." She looked toward the back door. "They're fixing to leave, if you'd like to say good morning."

"Are you sure there's nothing I can do?"

"Not right now. Go ahead—they're out back."

Sammie put her biscuit on a napkin and carried it out to the back porch along with her coffee. She stood in the shade, leaning against a post, and broke off a bite of biscuit.

Oh, my… Pure heaven. She made short work of the rest of it.

She sipped coffee, strong and good if lacking the chicory she was accustomed to, and watched the activity with interest. She'd never seen cattle worked before, though she was familiar with horses, having learned to ride when she was younger.

She left her coffee on the railing, and walked out in the yard, slipping out of the gate but standing well away from the action. The last of the cattle were being loaded. Case turned to take his horse back to the stable, and saw her standing there. He dismounted and walked his horse behind him, moving toward her with only a slight limp.

As he neared, her breath caught, her pulse raced.

He was larger than life, yet very…real.

So very, very…male.

Case had awakened early out of habit, surprised by a sense of optimism.

The red lingerie he'd had to remove from the shower rod had nothing to do with it.

And now there she stood, looking for all the world like a picture he'd never realized he'd carried around in his heart. Home at the end of a long day, your woman waiting to welcome you.

She made him all but stop dead in his tracks. Yesterday's short skirt had shown off one fine pair of legs, and her blouse had hidden little of her lush figure.

But this outfit, soft and sweet and old-fashioned, made her seem to belong here. No longer the city girl, the princess, now she looked a part of the land, the soft dark waves of her hair framing her face and flowing over her shoulders. The long skirt swayed gracefully with the movement of her hips as she walked.

And aren't you all flowery and sentimental?

"Good morning." He moved closer, stopping with bare inches between them, the toes of his boots planted on either side of her slender feet.

"Good morning." A smile curved her lips.

Caught up in the moment, Case tipped his hat back and bent to her, lured by the lush lips, savoring his memories of their taste.

"Whoo-ee, Case, so that's what's kept that shit-eatin' grin on your face all morning!"

Case didn't turn around. "Ralph, don't you have something productive to do, or am I gonna have to come over there and kick your scrawny ass?"

"Aww, no call to get all huffy. I was just kiddin'."

Wiley intervened. "Come on, kid, we've got to hit the road. You coming, Case? Good morning, Sammie." He tipped his hat.

Sammie smiled.

God, she was beautiful.

Case disregarded good sense and closed in on her to grab what started as a quick, friendly kiss. But when his mouth touched her soft, full lips, he knew in an instant that quick was not what he wanted. He placed one hand on her waist to bring her closer.

A little gasp. The faint press of her curves.

No, quick was definitely not going to do it. He wanted more…a lot more.

Shaken by how much he wanted it, he let her go.

"I wish you didn't have to go, Case." Her wistful tone warmed him.

"Me, too."

They lingered until Wiley started up the truck and revved the engine.

She stepped back. "Have a good time."

He hesitated. "You'll be okay?"

She smiled. "I'll be fine. Thank you for letting me be here."

They both sobered, knowing this was only temporary. Remembering that danger waited for her.

He tipped his hat to her. "I'll see you later."

"I'll count on it," she said in that dark chocolate voice.

Walk away. Now.

He did.

Barely.

She was still watching as they drove out of sight.

Sammie stood motionless until they left, then she turned to go inside, missing him already while knowing she shouldn't.

But he'd been there for her as no one else had since this nightmare began. Still, she shouldn't be counting on anyone. Her uncle's misdeeds weren't Case's problem. The little she knew about his situation told her that he had enough to juggle.

She had to figure this out herself. She pasted on a bright smile before she entered the kitchen and rinsed out her empty cup. "May I be of help, Linnie Mae?"

"Why don't you just rest today? Here you go." She gestured toward a chair and set down a full plate.

Sammie's appetite had waned. "I'm not used to idleness. I'd prefer to be useful, if you'll let me."

"I'll keep that in mind. You go ahead and eat now." She hesitated. "If there's someone you need to call, you go right ahead and use the phone. Even if you have a cellphone, coverage is pretty awful out here."

Sammie swallowed and kept her eyes on the plate. "I'll try my family later. They're not early risers."

She felt Linnie Mae's piercing gaze. She didn't like lying, but the warnings she'd received were clear. These people were solid and honest and kind, though. They deserved better than her lies. So did Case.

At last Linnie Mae turned back to the sink. "We're happy to have you here with us. I haven't had a woman around to visit with in some time."

Sammie forced herself to eat while listening to the older woman move around the kitchen.

"Sammie, I have to go to town this afternoon. Would you like to join me and pick up a few things to tide you over?"

Oh, dear. She couldn't let them spend money on her, but how on earth was she to come up with some when she didn't dare access her own funds? She only had what was in her purse, and it might have to last a long time. She couldn't imagine how she could earn the money for the things she needed out on a ranch in the middle of Texas. "Linnie Mae, I would but…"

"If it's the money you're thinking about, don't worry. Case gave me some cash and asked me to take you."

Sammie stifled a groan. "I don't want to take Case's money. I'll figure something out—please, just bear with me. I'm not used to having anyone take care of me anymore. I like handling my own affairs."

"Well, so do we all, hon, but sometimes we don't have any control over that. Case wouldn't offer it if he didn't mean it. Heaven knows he's got plenty of other uses for it." Turning back to her work, she muttered in a low tone.

All Sammie caught was *took off with all his money*. "What did you say—"

Just then David's wail sounded from outside. Wiping her hands on her apron, Linnie Mae rushed to the back door. After a moment's observation, she shook her head and smiled ruefully, returning to the counter.

The sound of the children's feet pounding on the porch, the slam of the gate, and their excited voices chattering and giggling made Sammie smile, too.

Raising two energetic grandchildren at her age must be hard, yet Linnie Mae was unflappable. An amazing woman, so capable and independent, yet Sammie had seen how deep the affection ran between her and Wiley. She couldn't have been more different from Sammie's mother, scared to say *boo* to her father. The atmosphere in which Sammie had been raised was so stilted and formal, so exacting. These people were warm and real. Sammie had sworn long ago she'd never be like her mother, a shadow at best, if a beautiful, elegant one.

Given the volume of the chatter outside, Sammie suddenly wondered how Linnie Mae had kept her from hearing the children last night and this morning. "I'm sorry you had to keep the children so quiet for me, Linnie Mae."

Linnie Mae looked confused, then smiled. "With those two, quiet is a relative term."

"But I never heard a peep from them. Is their room far away from the one I had?"

"About a quarter of a mile."

"A quarter of a mile?" she echoed.

"This is Case's house, Sammie. Ours is down the road."

She felt suddenly breathless. "Who else lives here?"

"No one."

"No one...you mean, Case and I... Ralph doesn't live here either?" Though that would be worse. Wouldn't it?

"Ralph lives in the hands' quarters next to the barn."

"But you...the meals..."

"This was the house Case grew up in. Oh, he wanted us to move into it before he came back, and then when the little ones came to us, he offered again, but Wiley and I have lived in our place for a long time. It's a bit crowded with the children, but it's home." She gave Sammie a sympathetic smile. "I can see how it would confuse you, but this was always where we fed everyone, back when Case's mother was alive and there were more hands. That's why the kitchen's so large."

Sammie mentally counted the rooms upstairs. Only one had been the bathroom. Almost afraid to ask, she ventured, "Is the master bedroom downstairs?" Visions of red lingerie on the shower rod flashed in her head.

"Oh, no, hon. That's the master bedroom you're in. Case still sleeps in his old room right across the hall from you. He refused to take over the master." She turned back to her work. "Case and his father didn't get along too well."

"He did tell me he left home at sixteen." Hesitating to pry but drawn to understand him, Sammie pressed on. "He said his father hated him, but surely..."

Sorrow crossed the older woman's face. "Jack Marshall was a difficult man. He was the black sheep of his family and had nothing to do with them after some big to-do when he was a teenager." She looked out the window then, as if another scene played in her mind. "He was never a happy man, I don't believe—certainly not during the time we knew him. Case's mother was about the only happiness he ever knew and the closest he came to settling down, but he was always restless, and after she passed when Case was just a boy…" She shook her head. "He buried his wife and abandoned his son, and that's the sad truth of it. He turned right back to drinking and gambling the way he had before he met her, and heaven only knows what he was doing when he was tomcatting around."

Her tone went bitter. "Even when he'd come back here, he never had a kind word for his boy. Knocked him around, too, I think, but Case would never say. As Case got older and bigger, he'd defend himself and had the size to do it. Black Jack sure didn't cotton to that. He didn't like not being king of the roost. Terrible way to treat his only son."

Her mouth pursed, then she continued. "One day Jack just went crazy on Case over something minor, and Case wouldn't back down. I swear one of them would have wound up dead if Wiley hadn't stepped into the middle of it—and he got a split lip for his efforts. Case was so appalled he left right then—" Her voice hitched. "And he never came back. If we hadn't wanted to watch over Case's legacy for him, we'd have packed up and left, too. Never thought much of Jack Marshall. Case was a fine boy and grew into a fine man. Jack should have taken care of that boy, not run him off."

She sighed. "Jack would never talk about it, but he had to know Case disappearing was his fault, and he seemed to lose interest in the ranch after that. After he died, this place was teetering on the brink of disaster. Not much of a heritage for Case."

"When did that happen?"

"Five years ago."

"How old is Case?"

"He just turned thirty-two."

Two years older than her. "Where was he all those years?" Sammie's heart ached at the thought of the young boy who'd grown up all alone.

"All over, honey. We didn't always know where he was, but he was good about checking in with Wiley and me now and again. It was only under the condition, though, that we not talk to Jack about him. Like to broke my heart that he never saw his father again before he died."

So much pain. What had it done to the young Case? How much did the grown man carry inside?

Linnie Mae wiped her hands on her apron. "Case is a good man who deserves better than what he's gotten. As a boy, he tried so hard to make his father love him, but Jack didn't know how to love anyone except maybe Case's mom." She exhaled. "And then it was too late for both of them."

Sammie didn't know what to say. Her father might be autocratic and her mother might be vague and uninvolved with her, but she'd always known that they cared about her. And she'd had every luxury handed to her on a silver platter. She'd had servants, expensive cars, trips to Europe.

And while she was being coddled and pampered, Case had been all alone, half-grown, fending for himself in God knows what kind of places.

Linnie Mae turned back, wiping off the counter with a sponge. "Case carries way too many troubles on those broad shoulders of his, and he won't accept help from anyone."

Sammie's heart quailed at the thought that she'd just added one more burden.

She'd better figure out something soon.

Chapter Seven

C ase ignored the auctioneer's chant as he waited for their
first lot to come up. Motes of dust swirled in the light,
stirred up by the livestock milling on the floor of the dirt ring.
He'd felt invigorated earlier, being back doing the work he
loved, but now the lack of sleep was taking its toll. He settled
back to wait, content to sit beside Wiley in a companionable
silence.

"Last time I saw Joe Bachman, he said he might have
something for you," Wiley offered.

Case's eyes narrowed as he wondered what his old buddy
might have uncovered about Roland Bracewell. Having a bank
president for a friend might be about to pay off with information. He and Joe had grown up together. When Case hadn't
been able to make enough headway on his own efforts, he'd
gone to Joe, who had volunteered to see what he could find
out about Roland Bracewell's whereabouts and history. Maybe
he'd found something helpful.

Wiley said casually, "I saw Joe in the cafe just now. I'll
stay here and keep an eye on our first lot if it comes up before
you get back."

Case made his way down the row and climbed the concrete steps from the auction ring, pausing several times to
exchange greetings with other ranchers. When he entered the
cafe, he spotted Joe Bachman in a corner booth. Joe waved

him over.

Case slid into the seat and gave his order for coffee to the waitress.

"How's it going, Case?"

"No complaints, Joe. How you doin'?" At Joe's nod, Case continued, "Sally okay? The boy?"

"Growing like a weed. You ought to try it sometime. Nothing like having a son—best feeling in the world when a little guy looks up to you like you're ten feet tall."

"You're a good father. No reason he shouldn't think that way."

"Well, I remember how it was with my dad when I was in high school. Didn't think the old man knew anything. It's really something—when you have kids, all of a sudden you realize that your parents might not have done everything right, but they did the best they knew how. Crazy business, being a parent—we don't get any training except on the job."

"Some parents need more training than others," Case observed. He couldn't help thinking of his father. Dark memories stirred. He tamped them down ruthlessly.

Joe paused as if realizing how tough this discussion must be on Case. His eyes revealed sympathy that Case didn't want. "Not all parents do so badly with their kids, Case. I bet you'd be a good dad."

"Well, that's not likely to be put to the test." Case didn't want to pursue the subject. "Wiley said you wanted to see me?"

"I do. You know I've been running a new retail credit report from time to time on Roland Bracewell, hoping he'd surface somewhere. After this long, I really didn't think we'd ever find anything."

Case nodded, intent on every word.

"Well, it just paid off. I got the new one, and there's been an inquiry from a bank in Tennessee."

"What does that mean?"

"It means that for some reason he's drawn their attention. Most likely, it means he's gone to them to borrow money, but it could be for other reasons."

"So where does that leave us?" Case asked.

"I can place a call to that bank and see if I can get an address on him, if you're sure you want that." He looked at Case intently. "Don't get yourself in trouble over this, Case. Turn it over to the law."

Case snorted. "Not hardly. I want to have a little chat with Roland first. The authorities can have their chance at him, but not until he's answered some questions for me."

"It's no good taking the law into your own hands."

He barely listened, his mind racing as he realized that he might have his day with Roland Bracewell, after all.

"Case—"

"Don't worry, Joe. I won't do anything stupid. I'm not ready to go to jail. I spend too much time away as it is. How soon do you think you'll have something?"

"I'll start making calls tomorrow morning, but I don't know how much I can turn up or how long it will take. Maybe I'll have something for you tomorrow, but it may take longer."

"I'd better get back." Case rose to return to the auction, stopping to clasp Joe on the shoulder. "Thanks, buddy. I owe you."

Case sat down beside Wiley without comment. Intent upon the bidding taking place, Wiley waited a minute for Case to speak. When he didn't, Wiley forged ahead.

"He have anything?"

"Maybe."

Wiley raised his eyebrows.

"We may know more in a day or two. Looks like he might

be in Tennessee."

"Son of a gun! What are you going to do?"

"I'm gonna have me a little chat with a man in a white suit. When I'm through, we'll see what happens," Case replied grimly.

"I'd be real glad to go with you."

"I know, Wiley. But this is something I have to do myself. I brought this bad luck down on us, and I've got to be the one to fix it."

"Just don't be foolish, son. Chances are the money's all gone, anyway. It won't help us hang onto the ranch if you're in jail."

Case knew that.

But it didn't matter.

"They're back!" Jennifer squealed and dashed outside.

Sammie hung back. She glanced down quickly at her new Wranglers, brushing a speck off the plain white t-shirt she had tucked inside. Linnie Mae had brought the outfit back from her errands in town in spite of Sammie's protests over spending Case's money. The older woman had guessed her sizes well. Best of all, she'd brought new underwear—made of serviceable cotton rather than the silk she normally wore, yes, but a heavenly change to Sammie anyway.

Sammie couldn't help being amused at herself. The only jeans she'd ever worn had been designer jeans, usually in a rainbow of colors with matching silk shirts. She didn't know the last time she'd worn a t-shirt, and she hadn't had cotton panties since she was a little girl, long before she needed a bra. If Papa could see her now, he'd be scandalized, but Sammie felt like a new person.

Wiley entered the kitchen and gave Linnie Mae a hug.

Then Case filled the doorframe. Her heart gave a funny little leap when he smiled at her and came her way. "How are you?"

"I'm fine, thanks." She hesitated. "I wish you hadn't given Linnie Mae the money, Case. Not that I'm not grateful," she hastily amended. "It's just that—"

"Not your style?" One eyebrow arched as he waited for her answer.

"Oh, no, it's not that at all. They could have been overalls, and I'd still be grateful. It's just..." She glanced away. "I feel funny about having you pay for them."

"I've had some times in my life where I only had one change of clothes. I didn't want you to have to live like that. I'm just sorry it's not something fancier."

"Oh, no, Case, they're wonderful! I'm thrilled, truly." She pirouetted before him.

Case's gaze traveled down her body, sizzling slow.

Then he spotted her feet and laughed out loud.

"What's the matter, you've never seen Keds before?"

"Not on anyone over the age of six."

"Well, I'll have you know lots of grown women wear them and do so happily."

"In bright pink?"

Sammie leaned closer, whispering, "You don't make fun of them, hear? Linnie Mae picked all of this out herself because I refused to go, thinking maybe she wouldn't spend the money if I weren't there. She thought the shoes would perk me up, and she was right."

"Linnie Mae—" Case turned toward the older woman.

"Case!" Sammie grabbed hold of one rock-hard bicep to stop him. It was like trying to move a mountain, so she sneaked her fingers under his arm and tried tickling him.

Case jerked away, then rounded on her, eyes gleaming with mischief. "Two can play that game, honey."

"No!" she shrieked and tried to get away. She was horribly ticklish.

His hands raced along her torso, tickling her ribs and moving toward her hypersensitive armpits. Sammie squealed in terror and scrambled to get away.

While giggling helplessly.

Everyone in the kitchen turned around. The children stood at the door, eyes round as saucers.

The silence in the room sank in on Sammie first as she tore around the table, trying to escape Case's nimble fingers.

She stopped, stock-still, warmth spreading from her neck to the roots of her hair. Case only grinned and shrugged.

The inhabitants of the room stared as if the two of them had grown extra heads.

Wiley cleared his throat, huge grin plastered over his face. "Well now, is anybody hungry?" His twinkling blue eyes shone.

Everyone began to move again. Case's grin subsided, but his eyes were still alive with mischief. Sammie busied herself at the kitchen counter.

Linnie Mae handed her a bowl to transport. "It's ready, folks. Have a seat." Her eyes were sparkling, too.

"It's more peaceful sitting by me, Sammie," Ralph said.

Case stared him down. "Her chair is right here." He pulled it out for her and settled her in it.

Ralph only grinned.

As the food made its way around the table and lively chatter accompanied it, she reminded herself that this sense of belonging was only temporary.

But it felt really good.

Case shifted beside her and drew her attention. A wicked grin flashed, but beneath it was the sizzle of desire.

Oh, he was lethal, even more so when he was playful. He knew it, too. On impulse, she stuck out her tongue at him.

He leaned over and whispered beneath the din, "I have better uses for that tongue than to taunt me, babe."

The deep, smoky tones made her shiver. She glared at him.

He only chuckled.

She ducked her head to study the food on her plate, unable to repress a smile.

Blissfully unaware of the charge crackling in the atmosphere, the children competed for attention to tell the details of their day, chief among them being the new kittens in the barn.

"Case, have you seen Missy's kittens?" Jennifer asked.

"Case, they can't see!" David fretted.

"Silly, they're just babies, like you. That's why they can't see," Jennifer taunted.

"I'm not a baby! Case, tell her I'm not."

"You're not a baby. The kittens' eyes will open soon, don't worry." Case turned to Jennifer. "How many are there?"

"Seven. Want to see them?" Her eyes gleamed with hope.

"Sure. How 'bout you show them to me after supper?"

"Okay!" Showing impressive big sister wisdom, she turned to her brother. "Want to help me show them to Case, David?"

His entire face lit up. "Let's go now, okay? Okay, Case?"

Linnie Mae intervened. "Case has been working all day. After supper will be soon enough—if you eat all your vegetables, young man."

His expression made it clear that David had to weigh whether the price of Case's attention might not be too high. "O-o-kay, Granny." He sighed heavily.

Sammie smothered a grin. Dinners at her home had been stiff, formal affairs. The girls were required to bring a topic to the table and report on it while maintaining perfect decorum. It was important to prove their readiness to enter the elevated circles in which their parents moved. This affectionate interplay was a breath of fresh air.

A few minutes later, Jennifer asked to be excused and rounded the table to Sammie's chair. "Come with us to see the kittens, okay?" Jennifer wheedled. "They're really cute and you would like them a lot."

David was not far behind, his plate—well, almost clean of vegetables, Sammie saw. "Yeah, Sammie! Come see the kitties!" He grabbed her arm and pulled. "Help me, Case! She's too heavy!"

Case chuckled. "Son, you've got a few things to learn about women." He turned toward her. "Are you up for a trip to the barn? It's one of our top tourist attractions." He leaned behind her, stage-whispering to David. "Just this one time, maybe I should carry her. Next time it's your job."

Jennifer giggled behind her hand. In the wink of an eye, the two were out the back door.

Taking one last sip of iced tea, Sammie rose. "After I help clean the kitchen, I'd love to see the kittens,"

"No, honey, you go on," Linnie Mae said. "Ralph here doesn't look like he's worked hard enough today."

Ralph's mouth dropped open, but a stern look from the older woman kept him quiet. "Uh, yeah, sure. I can help."

Sammie frowned, but Linnie Mae didn't budge. "Go on now. Those children have ants in their pants."

"All right," she conceded, then glanced at Case. "But I think I can make it out there on my own."

Case chuckled. "After you, then, madam."

The ever-present breeze lifted her hair as they made their way to the barn, shadows lengthening in the summer evening. The nights had their own music here: the occasional bawl of a calf, the trill of a bird, the soft nickering of the horses as humans approached.

The mother cat had found her birthing place in the hay-loft, back in one corner. David stood at the base of the ladder, jumping from one foot to the other because his big sister wouldn't let him climb up until Case and Sammie arrived.

Then they made a train on the way up the ladder: first Jennifer, followed by David, with Sammie right behind him, worrying that he'd fall.

Case chuckled from the floor. "He's made that trip a lot in his short life. He started practically as soon as he could walk."

She felt the heat of him behind her, a solid, steady presence that would have comforted her—if he didn't tempt her so much more. Flustered, she focused on David and resumed her climb to the loft.

The tiny kittens mewed in high, thin cries. Missy the mother cat merely stared at the humans, her feline eyes blinking slowly as her brood tumbled around her, some seeking nourishment, others replete.

"Can we pick them up, Case?" David asked.

"Hold out your two hands together, like this," Case demonstrated, cupping both hands, palms up.

David followed suit, as did Jennifer. Gently, Case picked up a kitten to place in each child's hands, then one in Sammie's. He moved his own hand beneath David's for security.

Seeing the tiny kittens in his large hands, Sammie shivered slightly, remembering those same hands fighting to protect her...stroking her tenderly... She recalled the feel of one strong hand at her waist just that morning, his touch all but claiming her. Her stomach fluttered.

There was a great well of kindness in him, a deep-seated protectiveness. Watching him with the children, she was certain that despite the poor fathering he might have received, Case would care for his own children well.

"Case?" Jennifer queried.

"Hmm?" Case kept his focus on David's hands and the kitten wiggling toward the edge of them.

"Do you think we'll ever get all our big trucks back?"

An instant of misery swept across his face, quickly erased. She recalled Linnie Mae's murmured words in the kitchen that morning and wondered if the two were related.

"I don't know, Jennifer." His shoulders were stiff. "I

hope so."

With a quick move, he caught the kitten falling from David's hands. "I think we'd better get these kittens back to their mama."

"Can't we pet another one?" David asked.

"I think we've bothered Missy long enough for now. Mamas get real protective." He ruffled the boy's hair before moving to help Jennifer put her kitten back.

Sammie followed suit, placing the black silky kitten she'd been petting at the mother's side.

"I wish they could come to our house," Jennifer said. "I would take good care of them."

Case gave her a quick hug. "I know you would, but Missy's a barn cat. She's not used to being locked up inside a house. She'll be happier here. Anyway, I think it's someone's bath time."

Groans greeted his announcement, and Sammie couldn't stifle a grin. The procession reversed itself, heading back down to the barn floor.

"I'll walk them back," Case said to her. "I need to visit with Wiley a minute, anyhow."

"Good night, Sammie." Jennifer clasped Case's hand.

David dropped his hold on Case's other hand and ran to her. Deeply touched, Sammie crouched and opened her arms to him.

"'Night, Sammie," he whispered, small arms squeezing her neck tightly.

Sammie's throat went tight. Jennifer ran over and leaned on her other shoulder, giving her a quick hug.

"Sweet dreams," the little girl said.

Sammie closed her eyes and squeezed both children. "Sweet dreams, you two. Thank you for taking me to see the kittens."

When they returned to Case's side, Sammie watched the tall man and the two small children walk down the road toward Wiley and Linnie Mae's, an unfamiliar pang tugging at her heart.

Later, Sammie felt his presence even before she heard the screen door close. She didn't turn from where she stood, leaning against one of the front porch columns, looking out toward the road. Twilight faded into darkness, and the scent of honeysuckle perfumed the air.

Neither spoke, the night sounds swirling amidst the currents between them. The air seemed more alive whenever Case was near.

And the house was empty of anyone but them now.

"Lovely evening," she ventured. "You have a really nice place here, Case."

The line of weariness that marked his frame shifted as he straightened, eyebrows lifting in surprise. "It's nothing like New Orleans."

She stared out at the stars. "It has a beauty all its own, just as you told me."

He surveyed the surroundings. "I hardly notice anymore."

"It's no wonder. You work too hard."

"Linnie Mae been worrying about me again?"

"Yes, but I have eyes of my own. You look weary to the bone."

"No help for that."

Talk to me about it, Case. She wanted to understand his problems, wanted him to share himself with her. Ironic, since she had shared next to nothing with him.

She had no right to pry, even if it were her nature. And she sure didn't want to cause him discomfort, after all he'd done for her. The best thing she could do for him right now was let him get some sleep. His exhaustion was almost palpable. "You've had a long day, Case. I'll let you get to bed."

A powerful urge to hold him close and offer comfort seized her. At the screen door, she stood for a long moment, one hand poised on the handle, wishing he would ask her to stay.

When he didn't, she hurried inside.

Sometime later as she lay in bed, unable to sleep, she heard his footsteps on the stairs, then the sounds of him moving about, getting ready for his own bed so very nearby.

They were alone. If she called out to him, he would come.

Neither would have to be lonely for this one night.

Guilt nagged at her for wanting to be held in those strong arms so much. Guilt for the problems she'd presented to him when he needed no more, for hiding the truth about why she was in trouble. For being tempted to ask for his help.

She had no doubt that Case would try, but not only would she place her family at risk by involving anyone else, she might place this kind and warm family in jeopardy, too.

She couldn't do that. The least she owed this good man was not to add to his burdens. She had to find her own way out of this mess.

A good man. Case Marshall was definitely that. A man who cared for a child's feelings, who rescued a woman he didn't even know. Who wouldn't give up on a failing ranch.

She couldn't help contrasting him with her former fiancé. Brant Gordon had been her father's hand-picked candidate for son-in-law: good pedigree, bright future at the bank, all the social graces. Perfectly prepared to entomb Sammie in a life just like her mother's.

She tried to imagine Brant leaping over the hood of a car, charging like a warrior to her rescue. She almost laughed. The picture wouldn't form. Brant would have to get his hands dirty.

Thank God she'd escaped that fate and sent Brant on his way, regardless of how angry her father had been. Marriage was a tomb, love the rock that sealed you inside. No way was she letting herself be sucked into that fate.

Flirting at the edge of her thoughts was the awareness that Wiley and Linnie Mae were still in love at their ages and neither of them seemed entombed. On the contrary, they seemed completely alive and vital.

As her eyelids drooped, one uncensored image flitted through her mind, a picture of Case with tender eyes focused on her...

Don't even think about it. There is no future for you here. You have to leave the second you figure out where to go.

As she slid into the inviting embrace of sleep, she thought she heard footsteps pause just outside her door.

Her last thoughts were wishes...for what could not be.

"We've found the trail, Mr. Gascoigne."

"Where?"

"Outside Snyder, Texas."

"You said the trail."

"Yes, sir."

"Where is the woman?"

"Uh, we're not sure yet."

"Why do you call me then?"

"I just—I thought you would want to know that we're close, sir."

"Raymond?"

"Yes, sir?"

"Close is nothing. Do not bother me until you have her. *Comprends?*"

"Yes, sir."

"And Raymond?"

"Sir?"

"I am distressed when two of my men cannot handle one young woman."

"But, sir, it's the trucker—he—"

"He is nothing, Raymond. Do whatever it takes to separate them. Just bring me the woman. I grow weary of your incompetence, and you know what happens when I grow weary…"

"I'll see to it, sir."

"You do that, Raymond."

Chapter Eight

The next morning as Sammie helped Linnie Mae clean up the kitchen, she struggled with the knowledge that she couldn't stay.

Astonishing to think that Samantha St. Claire would wish to do so.

She washed dishes as though she'd done it often, but she had to think hard to figure if she'd ever washed dishes by hand before. Certainly not when she lived at home; they'd had household help all her life. Even in her apartment, she'd had a dishwasher. Yet here, Linnie Mae worked as women must have done for centuries. She made her own bread, she raised a garden and canned vegetables, she hung the laundry to dry outside on a line.

It was hard work, no question about it. Sammie couldn't vouch for herself over the long run; maybe the appeal was simply the novelty of it.

But it felt good. Felt honest to work this way.

"Do you ride, Sammie?"

She jerked out of her thoughts. "What?"

"Do you ride horses?"

Cautiously, Sammie answered, "Yes, why?"

Linnie Mae frowned. "I'd like to ask you a favor."

Since Linnie Mae had yet to ask anything of her, Sammie agreed instantly, relieved to have a chance to repay this generous woman. "Of course."

"Case would skin me alive if he knew I was asking, but this is between you and me, all right?"

Sammie hoped it wouldn't be anything that would upset him.

"You could help me out by asking Case to take you riding. I can't remember the last time he had a day off. He won't take it easy if we urge him to do it, but he might, if you were the one asking."

Relief flooded through her, accompanied by a niggle of shame at her eagerness to have time alone with Case. "I'll be happy to try. I don't know if he'll listen to me either, but he does look really tired, doesn't he?"

Linnie Mae nodded sorrowfully. "He sure does, honey. The man could use some fun in his life."

When they finished, Sammie dried her hands and headed outside to look for Case. She found him beside the barn in the shade, cleaning the hooves of his horse. His shirt was off in deference to the heat, and Sammie's mouth went dry as she surveyed his lean, muscled torso, the dark hair spilling over his forehead.

She stopped in her tracks, drinking in the sight of him. Itching to touch him.

Case knew the instant she came near. Even if Comanche hadn't stirred at the presence of a stranger, he would have been certain. The air thickened. His body came alert.

He looked behind him.

She was several feet away, too far to reach out and touch.

But damned if he didn't want to.

He cleared his throat. Smiled. "Good morning."

The blue eyes crinkled at the corners as she smiled back.

"Good morning." The dark chocolate voice slid over his nerve endings, tantalizing even as it pleasured.

He went for casual. "Sleep well?"

"Oh, yes," she answered, a little too brightly.

Good. She felt the buzz, too.

"How about you?" she asked.

Not even trying to hold back the heat he knew was in his gaze, he responded. "Not as well."

"Oh, I'm sorry." Comanche stirred and drew her attention. "He's beautiful, Case."

"He's ornery as hell. Appearances can be deceiving." He felt obligated to issue the double warning. Comanche wasn't the only one who could present problems to her.

The brilliance of her smile surprised him. "I'm not afraid."

Need arrowed straight through him, the heat of the restless night climbing quickly to boiling again.

He forced himself back to Comanche's hoof.

"Case?"

That voice was driving him out of his mind. "What?" He knew he was too curt, but how was a man to ignore the sight of her, the scent of her…the sound?

She didn't speak for a long moment. At last she inhaled. "I know this is a lot to ask, but—"

Case waited.

"But?"

"Would it be too much to ask if you'd take me riding?"

This was way down on the list of requests he would have expected. "Riding?" He looked up quickly. "On a horse?"

That smile…sweet heaven, he could drown in that smile.

"Yes."

"You know how to ride?"

She rolled her eyes. "Even city girls can take riding lessons, you know." She paused. "So…would you? I know you're really busy, and I'll understand if you don't want to, but…" Her voice trailed off.

Case was surprised by how much he wanted to say yes. He looked around him, thinking of all he still had to accomplish today. He set down Comanche's hoof and stood up. He shouldn't indulge himself in the pleasure, but…he wanted to. A lot. "I still need to—"

Watching disappointment sweep over her face, he came to a swift decision. "If you could wait until this afternoon so I could finish up some things, I'd be happy to take you riding."

The brilliant smile that lit up her face swept away all his doubts. Maybe a few hours of pleasure wouldn't hurt. He'd make up for it later, if necessary.

But maybe, just this once, he could afford to lay claim to some time to play with this beautiful woman.

Sammie spurred Gypsy Girl, the bay mare he'd picked for her. "Race you to the tree!"

Case wasn't sure he wanted to win—the view from behind was pretty spectacular, whiskey curls flying behind her, shapely bottom teasing as she leaned over the mare's neck. Winning was rapidly falling to the bottom of his priorities. He'd already won, just being here with her on this beautiful day.

Then she cast a glance back over her shoulder and taunted, "What's the matter, cowboy? Aren't you afraid a city girl might beat you?"

He laughed out loud. Mischief—who'd have thought it? He used his thighs to signal Comanche. "Let's take 'em, boy."

Thanks to Comanche's powerful stride, they quickly pulled even, and the sight that greeted him almost took the breath right out of his body. No trace of city girl left, Sammie was pure warrior queen, alive and glowing with challenge. She melded with the mare to form one creature, her riding fluid and graceful. Her curls streaming behind her, Sammie looked his way, and the peal of her laughter lifted his heart. When she gave him an outrageous wink and spurred her mount, Case felt the warmth all the way to his boots.

No way he was going to rob her of the win. He got his reward in the gleam of her smile, the sparkle in her eyes. For the first time since he'd met her, the haunted shadows had retreated. Though he had a boatload of questions that still needed answering, Case decided to let the fragile peace stand as long as it could. He'd do a lot of things, if it would keep this Sammie alive and free. Unless he could see some sign that her troubles had followed her to the ranch, he'd let his questions be. As long as there was no danger to the people he meant to protect, he could wait.

The decision let a weight fall from his shoulders. Case dismounted from Comanche and moved to lift Sammie from her horse. Her arms slid around his neck, and he lowered her body slowly down the front of his. When her feet touched the ground, he didn't let go.

Every curve of her body seemed to warm and soften against him. Desire shoved all rational thought right out of his head. He lowered his mouth toward the lush beauty of her lips, knowing he shouldn't complicate things this way…knowing he should keep her at arms' length…knowing he couldn't care less.

His lips touched hers.

Comanche nipped the mare, and she shifted into Case.

Muttering, Case let Sammie go. "Goddamn troublemaker." He stomped around, grabbing Comanche's reins and moving him away from the mare.

Sammie giggled, and Case's ire vanished. Fun…he'd vowed to have fun.

He exhaled. Nodded toward the creek, grabbing the mare's reins where they'd fallen. "I'm going to water the horses. Want to see the creek?"

Sammie joined him. When they reached the water's edge, Case let the horses drink, separating them first. Once they'd drunk their fill, he led Comanche to a separate stand of grass. Neither horse would stray as long as he was nearby, but Comanche did better on his own.

Sammie took up a place beside him, looking around her curiously. "This is so pretty. Do you come here often?"

He picked up a flat rock and skipped it across the water. One…two… three skips it went, shooting up a fine tail of spray. He smiled, pleased that he hadn't lost the knack. "Not like I used to when I was a kid."

"You haven't forgotten how to skip stones, though."

"Some things just come back easily, I guess." He pointed to the large flat rock further down the bank. "I used to think that if I sat there long enough, I'd see the ghosts of the Comanches who used live around here."

"And did you?"

"Nope. But that didn't stop me from wishing."

"Was it lonely, Case? Being out here and being an only child?"

Being hated by my father, do you mean? He shoved the bitter thoughts away. "I don't know. I never had anything to compare it with. How about you? Are you an only child?" And here he'd just promised himself not to ask any questions.

She didn't answer immediately, but at last she did. "I have two sisters," she spoke quietly, almost as if she were afraid someone would hear her. "I'm the oldest."

Where are they? How old are they? How old are you? What were you like as a little girl? So many questions he'd resolved not to ask yet. "Want to walk up the creek a ways?"

She nodded, gratitude shining from her eyes.

They walked slowly, mostly in silence, punctuated only by the sound of the birds and the wind rustling the leaves. Case found a grassy spot under a big elm and lowered himself to the ground, sighing out loud as he leaned back on his elbows, long legs thrust out before him.

Sammie sat down beside him, legs crossed yoga style. Relief that he asked no more questions gave way to wondering what would have happened back there if Comanche hadn't nipped the mare. Trying to distract herself from that train of thought, she scanned the area.

"Were there really Indians right here?"

He'd laid down, his hat covering his face, his head resting in both hands crossed behind him. His answer was muffled by the hat.

"What?"

He pulled the hat away, setting it on the ground beside him. Sammie stared at him in frank appreciation of his dark good looks, the green eyes drawing her in, beckoning like the cool creek water sang a siren song to the hot, weary traveler.

"I said yes." Nodding toward the bluff just ahead of them, he explained. "That bluff was a great lookout point. You can see for miles from the top."

"Really?" Suddenly she wanted to see it. Glancing back to ask Case if they could go, she saw that his eyes had drifted shut, the lines of fatigue relaxing. She held her tongue, hoping that he might sleep.

It was certainly no hardship just to sit here and look her fill. A more beautifully made man, she was positive she'd never seen. The dark locks that so frequently spilled over his brow lay there now, tempting her fingers to touch them, to see if they were as thick and silky as she remembered.

He drew in a deep breath, and she saw him relax further. His breathing evened out, and she was almost certain he slept. Content to watch over him, Sammie settled in to enjoy her visual feast.

The same peace this place afforded Case crept into Sammie's soul. She emptied her mind of worries and questions, and soon she joined him in slumber.

Case's nose tickled.

He opened his eyes to see whiskey-brown curls waving, the wind lifting them to dance over his face. He wiggled his nose to dislodge them and wondered why he couldn't feel his arm.

It was a moment before he registered the warm flesh against his chest, the delicious bottom snug against his lap.

But it only took an instant for desire to consume his attention.

Damn, she felt good against him. His hand twitched, eager to fill his palm with her softness.

Then Sammie stirred. Sat up.

The release of her weight on his arm brought the sharp prickle of blood returning.

Case sat up, too, massaging to get the blood flowing.

"Sorry." Her cheeks were red.

He smiled. "No problem." To avoid grabbing her and kissing her senseless, he stood up. Looked toward the horizon, struggling against the urge to cover her with his body, to have her.

Now.

He grasped for something, anything that would deter him.

But he made the mistake of looking at her. He wished to hell she didn't look so damned sexy, her hair tousled as if she'd just arisen from bed.

His bed. That same bed he'd envisioned her in too many times since he'd watched her lick those luscious lips over coconut cream pie.

And now he could envision it so much more clearly. Could count how many steps away from that bed she slept.

How easy it would be to steal her from her own bed and draw her into his.

And then he was reaching for her, seeking the warmth of her mouth as though his life depended upon it.

Stop me, Sammie. For God's sake, stop me.

No way could he do it for her. Not now.

Sammie's mind had already gone a long way past no. If she'd thought that their encounter in the truck had been blown out of proportion by her memory, she knew now that memory hadn't even come close. She was aching, drowning…her every nerve alive, edgy need crackling.

Flexing her fingers on the taut muscles of his arms, Sammie slid her hands across his shoulders, burying her fingers in the thick black hair she'd been yearning to touch for what seemed forever.

She opened her mouth to him as she longed to open her body, her every sense straining toward him as though he were all that mattered in the world.

In that moment, it seemed that he was. She whimpered and stood on her toes, wanting to get closer.

The whimper registered on Case, driving the tiniest crack into the madness.

He grabbed for that minuscule breach, all too aware of just how close he was to taking her right here on the ground. His muscles quivered in protest, but he forced himself to let go.

It was now or never.

Even if they didn't have so much unsettled between them, so many reasons he couldn't possibly do right by her…even if Case didn't know to his marrow that this one woman could tear his heart apart if he let her in and then had to let her go…

Even if none of that were true, she deserved better than being taken, fast and hard, on the ground.

And there was no way he could be gentle, not right now.

He made himself step back, his breathing as rough as if he'd run a marathon. He forced himself to meet her eyes, then almost groaned aloud when he did.

Her eyes glazed, her lush lips kiss-swollen, her pretty breasts heaving, nipples hard and begging for his touch, Sammie's face was a study in confusion.

And he had no answers. So he only said "I'm sorry" and bent to retrieve his hat.

When he straightened, she had drawn her dignity around her like a cloak.

He felt the loss. The uncertainty of the next step.

Sammie solved it for him, more graciously than he deserved. "We'd better get back. I'd like to help Linnie Mae with supper."

Watching her walk away from him, Case damned his life, damned his responsibilities, damned his sense of what was right. With quick strides, he reached her side.

He grabbed her arm, and she rounded on him, temper flaring in her eyes.

"Sammie, it's not you. I just—so much is unsettled and I don't—"

"I understand. I'll be gone soon. It's better this way."

"Gone? Where are you going?"

She turned to her horse and didn't answer.

She didn't know, he realized. She could land right into trouble again. "Sammie, don't you do anything hasty. I can keep my hands off you. You don't have to leave."

Her head whipped around. Her eyes sparkled with an odd light. "You think I want you to stay away from me?"

"Don't you?"

Her smile became genuine. "Did I act as though I did?"

Okay, he was completely thrown off balance now.

"In the future, Mr. Marshall, you might remember—" She stepped into the stirrup, throwing her other leg over the saddle "—too much thinking can get you into trouble."

She flashed a smile over her shoulder and kicked her horse into a trot. "Last one home's a rotten egg!"

Fighting the urge to chase her down and drag her out of

the saddle, Case mounted quickly and set off after her.

Okay, so maybe she wasn't that fragile.

She wanted to be playful? Two could do that.

Tonight he'd take her dancing.

Who the hell cared if he was playing with fire?

He urged Comanche into a gallop.

Chapter Nine

At that evening's meal, Linnie Mae turned to Case. "I didn't get a chance to ask you yesterday how the auction went."

"It was good. Got a fair price, a little higher than I expected."

"But that wasn't the best thing that happened," Wiley added.

Every eye turned to the older man.

"You tell 'em, Case," Wiley urged.

Sammie couldn't wait to hear herself. She was so happy to know something good had come his way.

"Well," he began, "It looks like we may have a lead on Roland Bracewell."

Sammie froze. Roland Bracewell? Her *uncle*?

Before she could ask, Ralph spoke. "Seriously? You think you might be closer to finding that good-for-nothing sonofabitch?"

"Ralph," Linnie Mae warned.

Sammie's heart began to pound. What could—?

"Well, I, for one, hope you do," Linnie Mae muttered. "I'd like to get hold of that man myself for what he's put us through."

Oh, no. Sammie's gut clenched. *Please, no.*

"After he took off with all the money, he deserves a good

pounding, at the very least," Ralph said. "Promise me I can help you give him one."

The sound of her glass shattering on the floor grabbed everyone's attention. Sammie hastily bent to clean the mess, grateful for the excuse to keep her eyes on the floor, even as her mind raced.

Took off with all the money. Dear God. Shame flooded her. The very idea that someone related to her had hurt these wonderful people...

She desperately wanted to believe it was not her Uncle Roland, but somehow she knew it was. Thank heaven she hadn't told anyone any details about her life yet.

They would hate her. And they would deserve to.

Case knelt to help her while the rest of the group got up to clear the table. Sammie couldn't meet his eyes. "It's okay. I can take care of it." She heard her voice shake and fought for control.

Case lifted a jagged piece of glass out of her hand. "Let me help. Don't want to see those lady hands sliced up," he said gently.

She wanted to burst into tears on the spot.

Jennifer bounded around the table. "Don't worry, Sammie. I did that once, too, and I didn't get a spanking."

Sammie glanced up gratefully, then lowered her head quickly. It wouldn't do for anyone to see her distress.

She was too late. Case frowned as he saw her expression. Started to speak.

Before he could, Jennifer said, "We could go see the kittens again, if it would make you feel better."

Sammie couldn't help the little laugh that bubbled up. What was she going to do? Painful longing pierced her to the heart. She wanted to belong here. Wished she had nothing to hide from these kind souls.

Instead, now she had more.

She could feel Case observing her, then at last he spoke.

"Sorry, kids, I'm afraid we'll have to take a raincheck. I'm taking Sammie dancing."

"Dancing?" she echoed.

"Yeah, you know, we face each other and move around to music—you sure you're okay?"

How could she go dancing now? "*Dancing?*"

"Does that mean you don't want to go out with me?"

"No—I mean, yes, I'd love to, but—" Her uncle had destroyed his world, if she was understanding correctly, and he wanted to take her out.

Because he didn't know. Because she'd lied to him.

Misery swamped her.

He glanced behind him. "Didn't you tell me this morning that Miss Dolly was playing tonight, Ralph?"

"I sure did."

Case turned back to her. "Well, then, that's settled. Is it all right with you, kids?"

Jennifer goggled. "Sure, Case. She can see them tomorrow."

"But, Case, I don't—" She couldn't tell him like this. She didn't know how to tell him at all. Quickly she switched topics. "I don't have anything to wear."

His eyes crinkled. "What you have on is fine. Now go on and do whatever it is that ladies have to do, so we can leave."

"But—" She should tell him. Oh God, she had to think…

"Go on, Sammie. Time's a-wasting." With one hand on her waist, he nudged her toward the door.

She'd hardly uttered a word on the drive. She shouldn't be here. Wanted desperately to understand what her uncle had done and how she could fix it.

"We don't have to do this," Case offered. "I thought you

might enjoy it, but—"

She snapped back to the moment. "I'm sorry. I'm sure I will."

"Too back-of-beyond for you? I know it's not New Orleans, but—"

"No!" How could she let him think she was turning her nose up at anything when she was the one doing absolutely everything wrong? "I love to dance. I'm sure it will be great, but Case, maybe we should—"

He shut off the ignition and climbed out. Rounded the hood and opened her door for her. "We should have a good time. You said I needed to relax. Can't much do that if you're all wound up." He bent to her, his eyes going dark. "Of course, I'm kinda wound up myself, sweetheart."

His husky voice sent a shiver through her, and she grasped for the feeling of the afternoon and that lethal embrace.

He noted the shiver and smiled. Clasped her hand and led her inside.

The pulsating, sultry beat was one she'd felt throbbing through her body many times before. "Blues?" She looked up at Case in surprise.

He grinned at her astonishment.

When they found a table and sat down, Sammie looked around her. The clientele didn't look like the ones she saw in the Quarter, but everyone was clearly having a good time. Her gaze moved to the stage where the female singer, Miss Dolly, she supposed, dressed all in black, wielding a sinister-looking bullwhip.

Tight black jeans were topped by a black leather vest, and glimpses of a lacy black bra peeked through with each movement. The only relief from black was the brilliant crimson of her lips, the white of her bare arms, and her expansive cleavage. As she sang, her long, straight black hair swayed with her motions. She held the crowd in the palm of her hand, entrancing them with the rich, full power of her voice. She caressed the handle of the whip as she paused to introduce the next song.

"You know," her smoky voice purred, "Life is like a whip, soft on one end and...hard..." Here she paused and winked. "On the other. And just like a whip, life can cut you open...but if it's handled right, it can be a whole lotta fun."

The sly grin brought a tiny one to Sammie's lips as well, despite her misery.

Case watched Sammie, his gaze hot and promising. That slow, lethal smile shot sparks through her body.

But how could she let herself respond? How could she even allow herself to be here, having a good time, when her uncle had ruined Case's life? She thought about all the kind things he'd done. She desired him still, but he would hate her when he knew.

If only she could find some way to fix things for him... Nothing would erase what he'd been through at her uncle's hands, but she wanted so badly to make it up to him some-how.

She had access to great wealth, if only she could find her way out of the current morass. She would stop letting herself float in this lovely limbo of Case's world. She would find her uncle and bring him to justice. She'd make sure Case got back every penny he'd lost, even if it took every cent of her own money.

Once his business was made whole again, then maybe he and she could start over. See if they could have a chance to explore whatever this was between them, free of shadows and secrets.

It was the only way she could live with herself. The only way she could allow herself to stay here with this man tonight. The fixes she intended to make wouldn't take away what he'd been through, but maybe, just maybe...

Case grasped her hand and pulled her toward the dance

floor.

Her heart a little lighter for her resolution, she let Case draw her near.

Don't think, just dance. Don't spoil this night. It may be all you ever have with him.

Case walked her across the dance floor to a point near the stage. He could sense the worry still vibrating through her, but he was determined that they would have this night. He didn't understand why she'd gone so ashen earlier. He couldn't help his sense that there was something more than a broken glass at stake, but searching back over the conversations at the table, he couldn't remember anything that could have upset her, except finding out that he didn't have any money left, but hell, he'd told her that himself.

He shoved those thoughts away and focused on Sammie, not exactly a hardship. She wore her newly-clean miniskirt again, about a mile and half of leg showing, and she'd paired it with the pretty ruffled blouse Linnie Mae had loaned her.

He watched her relax inch by inch, and soon her hips were swaying to the primal, bluesy backbeat. Her eyes went sultry, her body was grace and sensuality wrapped up in one gorgeous package.

Okay, sure, he wanted to do way more than watch. His body strained for hers, and if he truly meant to keep his hands off her, coming here was a big mistake.

Then Sammie lost herself in the insistent, demanding beat. Threw caution to the winds and moved closer, her thighs brushing his, grazing the denim with slow strokes as she swayed to the music.

Sweet heaven. Violent need shuddered through him. With her head thrown back to expose her long neck and her whiskey curls flowing down her back, she was definitely wet dream material. His palms itched to cover the full breasts teasing him with their nearness. *If she rubs my leg one more time, it's all over.*

"Hey, Case, baby." They were startled out of the trance when his name was purred from the stage.

Dolly grinned like a Cheshire cat, slowly licking her lips while she stared straight at him and crooked her finger.

Case just grinned and shook his head no, turning back to Sammie.

Sammie was watching Dolly.

Dolly spotted her then, forehead wrinkling, gaze taking in Sammie in one insulting scan, eyebrows lifting as she looked back at Case.

Then her musical cue sounded, and she began to sing again, that throaty, powerful voice bent on seducing every man in the room.

Sammie stared at Case.

He just shrugged his shoulders and grinned.

She turned her back on him. Took a step away.

He grasped her hips. Bent to her. "Don't go. It's nothing. A long time ago."

She looked over her shoulder at him, then tossed her hair and sniffed. "I couldn't care less."

He couldn't help a pleased grin. "Liar." Damn, she was tempting. Since the music was too loud for conversation, instead he moved closer, rubbing her body with his, reveling in the feel of that delicious bottom sliding across the hardness straining at his jeans.

And he scowled at Dolly.

She broke into a big smile and scolded him with one long, scarlet-tipped finger.

Then Miss Dolly and the Devils segued into a slow song, and Case turned Sammie around into his arms. As he drew her close, she sank against him, laying her head against his chest as he drew their entwined hands next to his heart and laid his cheek upon her hair.

Bodies close, hearts drawing closer, the two gave themselves up to the spell of the music. The song spoke of love and loss, spinning a web of bittersweet glory around them. Beyond the insistent thrum of desire never far away when they were together, beyond all the reasons to keep them apart, something tender and young sprouted from the fertile soil of their passion. For the moment, they let it free to seek the sun.

When the song ended, they simply stood there, still as statues, caught in the moment. The emotion.

Then the band launched into a rowdy number called "You Can Take My Husband But Don't You Touch My Man."

The spell evaporated.

Sammie and Case returned to their table.

Sammie excused herself to go to the ladies' room. Once inside, she sagged against the wall.

Le bon dieu. The man turned her inside out. Guilt fought with yearning. Need battled with shame. She wanted so badly to yield to his powerful allure, to let that gorgeous hard body take her over, to feed the demand that grew by the day...

But her conscience wouldn't let her.

She had so much to hide. He made her feel too much.

Want too much.

She absolutely could not afford to get involved with this man while her life was in such chaos.

And he deserved better.

How she longed to return to the cool, dispassionate woman she'd been. Life had been so tranquil. If she was ever to solve her problems and return to any semblance of normal life, she had to get a grip on herself when it came to Case Marshall. She could do neither of them any good if she lost her head in longing for him.

Strengthened in her resolve, she emerged from the restroom, threading her way through the crowd back to their table.

And there was Miss Dolly bent over Case's chair, her arms wrapped around his shoulders as she leaned to whisper in his ear, breasts brushing the arm he had draped along the back of Sammie's chair. Their posture spoke volumes about past intimacies, and a sharp pain pierced her heart.

No. This was good. She needed anything that drew her back from the cliff's edge that was the very sexy Case Marshall.

As she walked around Case's other side to get to her seat, he straightened in his chair. Dolly was slower to remove her body from his, trailing her fingers slowly across his broad shoulders while casting a sly glance at Sammie.

Sammie's chin rose a notch in defiance.

Dolly only grinned while addressing Case. "Well, sugar, I guess I'd better be getting back. Due back onstage pretty soon." She grazed Case's lips with one long red fingernail. "It's been too long, lover. Don't be a stranger." With that, she turned and strolled away, the cool curves of her almost bare back amplifying the effect of swaying hips that drew the eyes of every man in the room.

Every man except one. Case had the good graces to look embarrassed, but it was better that she'd been reminded of the power he exerted over women, all too evident in the admiring glances he drew everywhere they went.

"Sammie..."

She needed air. Had to clear her head. Turning on her heel, she sought the door outside. Had to get away from all the confusion, the emotions roiling through her.

As she pushed through the crowd, an arm reached out to

stop her. She shrugged it off, still intent upon the door.

The man spoke to her, but all Sammie wanted was to escape from the hot, noisy press of bodies. As she emerged into the night, blindly headed into the parking lot, the incident with Dolly brought home forcefully how little she really knew about Case. She had been so afraid of Gascoigne and what he would do that the comfort the ranch and its inhabitants provided had lulled her into complacency.

Complacency spelled danger.

A hand on her arm whipped her around.

There stood a stocky brute much like the man who'd shoved her into his car at the truck stop.

A scream bubbled up in her throat.

His voice slurred, "Hey, pretty girl, come on back inside with me. It's been a long time since I held a woman like you." He dragged her toward the door.

"No!" She smacked at him, struggled to get free, panicked by her memories. Frenchy's fist...his brutal hands all over her...

"Hey, now—none of that, babe." He clamped her more tightly, a strong beery aroma wafting over her.

Had they found her? She tumbled back into the terror, fighting to breathe, suffocating under the weight of her fear.

"What the hell—?"

"Let her go."

The arms dropped away.

Panicked, she whirled and ran, the shouts behind her barely registering.

Strong arms seized her, pulled her close.

She screamed.

"Sammie, hey, now. Sammie, stop. It's me, it's Case."

His voice finally penetrated her panic. "Case?"

"Yeah, it's me. Are you all right? Did that drunken idiot hurt you?"

Every word brought her one step closer to sanity.

"A…drunk? Not—"

Case cursed. "You thought it was those men."

Shaken that she'd let her fear propel her into the wrong conclusion, she looked around. All she could see was a small crowd curiously observing her. One man stood in front, rubbing his jaw and shaking his head. She thought she heard the words *damn crazy woman* before he wheeled and headed inside.

Sammie turned away from Case, embarrassed but still trembling from the forceful reminder of her precarious situation. This incident might have been a false alarm, but it served as a vivid inducement to recall Gascoigne's warnings. Case would despise her anyway, as soon as he knew her connection to Uncle Roland. Just one more reason to remember that her sense of the ranch as a haven was a fantasy, nothing more.

As Case approached her again, she was already composing her necessary lies.

He spun her around to face him, eyes glittering. "Tell me," he growled. "No more delays, Sammie. I want to know about this man you're running from."

She closed her eyes to blot out the sight of his face, but the memories she held couldn't be erased so easily. Only knowing that she had to protect him from more suffering gave her the strength to be convincing.

"I've been involved with a man who is very possessive of me." She drew in a shuddering breath as she spoke. "He is obsessive about it and had me followed everywhere."

Her voice gained strength as she caught up the threads of her tale. As long as she didn't look at Case, she thought she could pull this off. "He's a powerful man, and a very determined one. He had me completely isolated. The only time I wasn't followed was when he was with me."

She blessed her voracious habit of reading suspense novels. She was borrowing heavily from plots she'd read. She only had to convince him until she could get away—which would be very soon.

"One night I managed to slip a sleeping pill into his drink, and he slept more soundly than usual. I made it out of his house and left New Orleans heading west, until my car broke down. You know the rest."

He watched her closely, searching her gaze. "And those goons who tried to take you were his."

She nodded, unwilling to speak.

"Why wouldn't you tell me this before?"

"It's not your problem, it's mine. I'm sorry I held back—I was afraid. I didn't have anyone to turn to who could help."

"Couldn't someone have helped you? Family? Friends?"

She mentally crossed her fingers, praying he'd believe her. "I don't have any family but my sisters, Case, and they—that is, we don't—" Tears flooded her eyes. For all intents, that much was true. She might as well not have any family, since she didn't dare contact them.

Case was silent for a long moment. She tilted her head up to see sympathy in his gaze. Feeling worse than ever about deceiving him, she looked at the ground. Wrapped her arms around her waist to hold herself together.

He drew her to his chest and laid his cheek against her hair, exhaling a long breath. "We'll figure something out. Come on, Sammie. It's been a long day. We can think about this tomorrow when we're rested. Let's go home."

Home. She had no home. She would have none until this was over.

But gratefully she accepted the reprieve.

Chapter Ten

Case awoke with a start. Rolled over, wondering what noise had speared through his exhaustion to wake him.

After the long emotion-filled day and the night of dancing, he'd fallen into a deep sleep, trying to forget Sammie's haunted face, trying to figure out the next step. He squinted at the clock. Just after two. He fell back onto the mattress, closing his eyes.

He heard it again. A whimper?

Sammie.

He sat up just as the whimper turned into a scream of pure terror. He bounded out of bed in a flash, not caring that he was stark naked. He raced across the hall to her room, cursing that he had no weapons at hand.

He charged through her door, half-expecting to see the thugs holding her hostage.

She was alone. Caught in another nightmare. Thrashing from side to side, kicking out and whimpering for help.

He sat and gathered her into his arms, using both his voice and his hands to calm her. "Sammie...Sammie...it's me, Case...you're okay. You're safe...wake up, honey." Slowly he stroked her back with his hands.

At last her breathing began to slow. Her eyes opened. "Case?" She lifted her hand to his cheek.

Her skin was warm silk. "Yeah, it's me. You're okay now.

It was only a bad dream." A sliver of moonlight slanted in where the shades had been left partly drawn to catch the breeze. In the dim light, he couldn't make out the color of those eyes he knew were blue, but their call was powerful.

For a long, hushed moment, the two of them stilled, eyes locked in taut, breathless wonder. Suspended between what was wise…and what was inevitable, longing demanding to be denied no more. With a sense of relief, of bowing to the inescapable, Case yielded to the temptation that had gnawed at him every minute since he'd last kissed her. Reverently he bent to her full, soft mouth.

Sammie's lips parted without hesitation, her tongue swirling smoothly along his. At once he deepened the kiss and brought her closer, draping her body across his lap, the cotton shift riding up and baring her sweet rounded bottom to his touch. His body stirred beneath her smooth flesh. She squirmed as though craving more contact.

Case was all too aware that he was naked.

And that she was not nearly naked enough. The thin cotton frustrated him, and only a hair-thin veneer of control prevented him from ripping it away. With her every wiggle, his desire for her surged. He might not need the complications she presented, but the time for waiting was past. He wanted her. He'd lose his mind if he couldn't have her right now, this instant.

He cast away his doubts as he surrendered his will, falling back on the bed, bringing her down with him. Writhing together in a torturous dance as old as time, her body skimmed over his, their legs entwined.

Sammie rose above him, splendid and sleek. Gliding up his body, she straddled his hips, her breasts full and tempting, just beyond the reach of his mouth. His tongue traced a line along the tender inside of her elbow, lapping up precious tastes of her skin. She gasped, and he smiled. His hands smoothed over her back, drawing her forward and caressing the firm globes of that sassy behind he so admired.

"Sammie…" he groaned. He squeezed the sweet flesh and she squirmed again. Her legs parted still more, bringing the small patch of red silk between her thighs into intimate contact with his length.

Case thought he might die. He wasn't sure he'd mind.

It would surely be the sweetest death imaginable.

Crazed for her now, he took one thinly-veiled nipple in his mouth while he sought entrance to the heaven she promised. She moaned and rocked her pelvis, torturing him with the feel of wet, heated silk. His teeth plucked at the thin shift, then his hands stripped it from her. He licked a scorching spiral around the sensitive aureole of one full, creamy breast. Hot, edgy need ground at him, and he grazed the erect nipple with his teeth, then slid into suckling her, drawing deep on the endless pool of sensuality shimmering beneath her surface.

Sammie trembled at the desperate wanting Case aroused. It wasn't just his killer good looks—he was so much more. She hadn't figured him out by a long shot, but she'd never met a more intriguing man in her life. For this one night, she would not think about how impossible it all was. She needed this closeness; she craved his magic.

So she yielded to him, to the driving, endless yearning. He called forth a wildness she'd never known was inside her, his every caress so deeply erotic, so intensely seductive.

Powerful magic he wielded, drenching her every cell, suffusing her every thought. She wanted only to feel, to burn…to surrender.

Case's impatient flesh prodded at her slick warmth, eager to slip into the paradise he knew he'd find. His fingers itched to rip the offending panties away, to plunge into her with no delay—but ruthlessly he battled back the primal, razor-sharp need.

And realized he had no protection with him.

He fell back with a groan.

"What's wrong?" she whispered, tensing. "Don't you want—?"

He met her eyes. "Babe, I want you so badly I hurt, I just—I'll be right back. I don't have anything with me." He let how he burned for her show. "Don't move one inch."

Her face relaxed into a dangerous smile. "I'm going nowhere, cowboy."

"I don't know. You have a habit of disappearing on me." He scooped her up and strode to his room. "I'm taking no chances." And the last place he wanted to be making love was in that room he still thought of as his father's.

He laid her on his mattress as if she were delicate crystal. He rummaged in his chest of drawers and came up with a string of packets. Opened one and tossed the others on the nightstand.

Sammie's laugh was low and throaty. "I like your ambition."

He grinned and joined her, ranging over her to explore more of her succulent, glistening skin, every second with her drawing him deeper under her spell. "Do you have any idea how beautiful you are?" he muttered, barely coherent, riding the rim of madness. He buried his fingers in the tangle of whiskey curls, scraping his teeth along the column of her neck. "I tried to stay away…tried, damn it." His patience strained to the snapping point, he lapped his tongue over her skin, nipped and teased her with his teeth, his lips, his hands, loving how she writhed beneath his touch. How she keened for release.

He paused to let his gaze scorch a trail over the beautiful contours of the woman who embodied every dream he'd ever had.

Lying across the bed, dark curls a rippling wave across the sheets, a sheen of sweat glimmering on her skin, she tore at every last shred of control he possessed. She was every bit the wet dream he'd imagined when he'd watched her tantalize him with a bite of coconut cream pie.

She dazzled him. His hands and his mouth roved restlessly over her body, teasing her sensitive skin and drawing her ever higher as he made his way to take the taste he'd promised himself when he'd watched her eat that piece of pie. He slid the silken panties slowly down her long, gorgeous legs and parted her dark curls with a slow, soft, whispering hot breath at their crown.

When he put his mouth to her, she moaned aloud.

Case redoubled his sensuous torture, not escaping the delicious, needle-sharp pain himself. Letting his fingers glide over her skin as his tongue licked and delved, he wondered who would beg first. When she rocked toward him, thighs trembling, silently begging for release, he took mercy upon them both and sent her on a scorching journey along the stairway to paradise.

Surely she had died. Was it possible to experience such rapture and live? she wondered. The pieces of her had tumbled onto a whisper-soft cloud and she no longer cared whether she was alive. If there was anything left of her mind.

But Case wasn't done yet. Once more he drew her up into a craving so sharp that she cried out. Opening her eyes, she saw him, her dark angel, hovering over her, his every line taut with blatant hunger. Talons of greed clawed into nerves raw with need. She dug her nails into his back and arched her body into his, ready for the climb.

Case saw her eyes blaze, the hunger in them naked and voracious. She wrapped her legs around him, urging him near. A fine madness sang in his heated blood.

No more waiting. Even if he could, he was through trying. After a journey that seemed years long since he'd first laid eyes on this magnificent woman, Case entered heaven in a single thrust.

What he felt at that moment needed better words than he

possessed. Bliss—yes. Rapture—of course. Exquisite torture.

But there was more, a feeling that for the first time in his life, Case Marshall had come home. After years of wandering, of desperate searching, years of lonely, angry longing, he had arrived at this unexpected place of belonging.

Shaken to his core, Case blessed the fire that quickly burned away any ability to think.

He clasped her hands in his, fingers interlaced. "Look at me," he commanded.

She was helpless to defy him, even if she'd wanted to— but she didn't. She wanted to drown in this dark desire, this firestorm of burning, raging need. They began to move as one, and Sammie experienced explosive passion for the first time in her life.

She finally understood why people were willing to die for love, what the poets meant when they spoke of a grand passion. This was surely the most powerful moment of her life.

Then she thought no more. Case demanded her total involvement, his potent pull undeniable. Hot, clawing need...sheer, crystalline glory...she was one with him, helpless to evade his magnetism. As he towered above her, calling her to himself like a sorcerer, she thought how pale and insipid were the men she'd known before. He could be the devil himself, and she would enter hell willingly and eagerly by his side. She abandoned herself to follow him wherever he wanted to go, knowing already that she could— and did—trust him with her life.

"Come now, Sammie," his rough velvet voice urged. "Let go. Fly with me." Releasing her fingers, he clasped her head in his hands, mesmerizing her. He stroked deeper and harder as she opened herself to him, willing her with a look to take it all.

The summit, when they reached it, was a place neither had known before. Blinded by starbursts...shaking with pleasure...drifting in silent wonder, they slowly spiraled down together, knowing they had truly touched the pinnacle of bliss.

Then, in a delicious, sweet languor, they held one another close, against the dawn to come.

"Case?" Sammie spoke into the side of Case's chest, curled up against him.

"Hmmm?" He drifted, at peace in a way he hadn't been in longer than he could remember.

"I'm hungry."

A laugh burst from him. He lifted his head and peered at her. "Again?"

She punched him lightly in the side. "Not for that, silly." She paused. "Though there are all those packets…"

Case groaned and fell back on the pillow. "You're going to kill me, woman."

"I don't think so. You look too strong. Me, now, that's a different story. I may faint from hunger if I don't get some food soon."

"Can't have that. Come on, you lightweight. Let's go rustle up some grub." Case sat up.

She grabbed him around the waist from behind, pressing a loud kiss to his backside. Arms tight around his belly, she spoke, "Case?"

"Yeah?"

"I've never…it's never been like that for me before."

He twisted around and leaned on his elbow. Studied her.

"Me either, sweetheart." He brushed his thumb across her lips. "Me either." He had no idea what to do about this unexpected gift. Or its complications.

But he wasn't one to dwell. He shook his head and smacked her bottom lightly, then rose. "Out of the bed, lazybones. The food's not going to march up the stairs, you know." When she made no move to follow, he turned.

She looked sad and lost. He returned to her and enfolded her in his arms, rocking her from side to side, his cheek resting on her hair.

She relaxed against him, and it felt so damn good. He wanted to fall right back into bed and tell the world to go hang.

But she was hungry, so after a quick hug, he turned her around and marched her into the hall.

"Case! I'm not going downstairs naked. Wait a second while I get—" She stopped, and he realized she didn't exactly have an extensive wardrobe to choose from.

"How about one of my shirts?"

"Thank you." She followed him back into his room, looking around curiously as they entered.

He wondered what she saw. It was a smaller room, the one he'd had as a boy, and spare in its décor, the king-sized bed dominating the space. It wasn't a place in which he spent much time. When he'd come back, he'd cleared out the remnants of his boyhood but had done little else to it beyond buying a new bed.

"Don't you want the master bedroom?"

"No." He saw her flinch from his sharp tone. "Sorry. It feels too much like my father's room, even though Linnie Mae redecorated it a few years ago."

He pulled a crisp white shirt from the hanger and held it open for her. Once her arms were in the sleeves, he moved in front of her and worked the buttons himself.

It was impossible, however—not that he tried—to resist pausing between each one to trace his hands under the fabric, stroking her curves and stealing caresses.

She was so responsive. As he bent and cruised his mouth down her throat, she squirmed. Sighed. Her nipples rose to tight points against his palms.

She was killing him. "This shirt has never looked so

good." Even he could hear his voice rough with need.

Sammie swayed against him, and he wrapped one arm around her waist. Bent his head to her.

"Oh, Case..." she sighed, going pliant in his arms.

They would be right back in bed in no time flat.

But she'd said she was hungry. She was too damn thin already.

He made himself step back. "I promised I'd feed you." Somehow he found the resolve to turn away and pick up his jeans.

"Oh, you are so gorgeous," she sighed.

He closed his eyes. "If you want food, you'd better move that pretty ass right now." He turned to see her face a tangle of longing and growing mischief.

"I'm going," she said with a smile. Outside the doorway, she glanced back. "Race you!"

And charged down the stairs.

He couldn't help grinning. He pounded down the steps behind her.

And let his heart float as he heard her breathless giggle.

There was a reckoning to come, he knew that. But right this minute, he wanted this peace, this fun, for however long it could last.

The light over the kitchen table caught them within its warm glow, creating a magic circle, a world in which they seemed the only inhabitants. Spread before them were the makings for giant sandwiches which Case demonstrated his skill in creating.

"I know I said I was hungry, but I'm not a lumberjack." She wondered how she would even take a bite out of the one he'd just placed in front of her, much less eat the whole thing.

Case's eyes gleamed. "Babe, I'm very aware that you're not a lumberjack. Never met one, but I doubt they have such soft skin or those sweet curves."

She couldn't help smiling but kept her eyes on the monster sandwich falling out of her hands. She took her first bite, hoping it wasn't too terrible, since he was so proud of himself. "Wow. That's actually good."

He grinned broadly. "Told ya."

At last he settled beside her and dug into his own. Sammie marveled that Case could eat such huge portions and stay so fit but chalked it up to the physical demands of his life. For herself, she knew she'd better watch the size of her portions or figure out some way to work them off. She smiled as she thought of all the calories they'd expended earlier in his bed, but the smile turned quickly to a frown as she remembered that her eating habits were the least of her problems.

Case saw the change in her expression. "You're worrying about him again. Don't fret—you don't have to leave anytime soon."

She couldn't meet his eyes. The tangle of her life wouldn't be held at bay forever. "I still have to figure out where to go from here."

"But not tonight."

Was that true? Was it fair?

His gaze compelled her, and at last she shook her head. "Not tonight." Relief suffused her, however temporary. She yearned to forget that there was anything in the world but the two of them. She couldn't hold off reality forever, but she very badly wanted the gift of this one night with Case before the world intruded.

Selfish? Absolutely. But he clearly wanted the same.

By tacit agreement, they rose to clear away their mess without speaking. When they finished, they strolled back to the hallway, arm in arm. Case surprised her by sweeping her off her feet and climbing the stairs with her cradled against his chest. She wanted to protest—he still limped slightly. But touched to her soul by his gesture, Sammie decided that Scarlett O'Hara was a fool. How could she have let go of a man who would do something this romantic?

When his mouth descended to hers, it was her last coherent thought for the night.

Chapter Eleven

C ase walked into the bank the next day in response to Joe Bachman's call. He was eager to hear what Joe had to say about Roland Bracewell.

Sammie had still been asleep when he left. She'd barely stirred when he'd risen from the bed. Knowing she must be exhausted from a night with almost no sleep, Case had let her be, though he'd wanted badly to touch her again.

But touching, he knew, would lead to more.

She'd been everything he'd ever dreamed of in a lover. Ravenous, tender, willful…giving and demanding as though she couldn't bear not to share every moment to its fullest. Just thinking of the heat and the softness of her, the way she came apart in his arms, made him want to turn his pickup around and head straight back to her.

If only…

But there were serious matters to tend to for them both. Like hunting down Roland Bracewell.

Once in the bank, Joe greeted him immediately. "Come on into my office, buddy. I think you'll be pleased with what I've found."

Case didn't want to waste time sitting, but he forced himself to do so, leaning forward, focusing on Joe and his news.

"Well, it appears that our boy's been traveling around, but he stopped in Nashville and opened an account with Builders

Bank. I can't get the exact figure, but there's somewhere around fifty thousand in that account."

Fifty thousand dollars. Not much compensation for the trucks and income he'd lost, but it represented the better part of what Roland had taken from the till.

"Where is he now?"

"I'm afraid I don't have that yet. I haven't run across any sign that he's living there. The address he gave on his account was one in New Orleans, and I heard an interesting tidbit from my buddy at Builders. Roland told him he used to be a banker in New Orleans—he ever say anything about that to you?"

Case shook his head. Their loan had come from Restoration Bank in New Orleans—the loan they'd had to default on when Roland took a hike. Strange that the same city kept coming up in his life.

"Want me to call a pal of mine at Restoration Bank and see what I can find out?"

"Yeah. Thanks." As he waited for Joe's call, Case glanced idly around the room, his mind skimming over conversations he'd had with Roland.

Case had a good friend of his own in New Orleans, one who moved in a world no banker would.

Joe hung up. "Huh."

"What?"

"Didn't you tell me your truck loan was from Restoration?"

"Yes. Why?"

"Well, it appears that our boy Roland was indeed a banker at Restoration, though many moons ago. He's got quite a colorful reputation in the Crescent City, it seems, and he's got some interesting relatives. His sister is married to the president of Whitney National Bank. Old-line establishment—old money folks."

Case didn't care about Roland's relatives unless they could

tell him where to find the bastard, but he forced himself to be patient and listen.

"Seems there's a lot of talk going on in those circles right now because Roland's niece has disappeared—just dropped out of sight a few days ago. My contact was concerned because he knows her. She's a banker, too—worked with him at Restoration. He said that it's being handled very hush-hush because it smells to high heaven. Her father is afraid it's a ransom attempt. High profile family. Garden District home, beautiful daughters, the works—go figure. The only trace of her they've found so far was that her Porsche was sold to a used car dealer in Houston who says the woman seemed nervous. And get this—she traded that Porsche in for an old sedan that turned up abandoned near Abilene. Somebody at a truck stop recognized her picture."

Abilene?

Abandoned car?

Recognized her picture at a truck stop, the beautiful daughter of a wealthy New Orleans family…

Only my sisters and we're not close.

Case's stomach churned.

No. No way.

Roland's *niece?*

Hadn't he'd known she'd been holding back on him? He thought about how jumpy she'd been, how evasive. He heard again the false notes in her voice last night.

Abruptly he remembered her face turning white when she broke the glass at the supper table.

After they'd mentioned Roland.

And Sammie was afraid of the police.

Every memory was a punch to the gut. He barely listened to anything else Joe had to say. His mind was in turmoil, trying to make sense of it all. Out of all the people in the world he should rescue…

If she didn't have anything to hide, why hadn't she spoken up? Was she a part of Roland's scam? She had a family looking for her, so why would she tell him that cock-and-bull story? Why would she say she had no one to help unless she, too, was on the run like Roland?

Good God, what had he done?

He'd brought the serpent into Paradise.

Rage simmered. What did he really know about this woman besides her sweet, soft skin, her inviting curves? Had he been so blinded by her beauty that he didn't see through to the rotten core? How many times had she dodged his questions?

There's this man...

Not only dodged. *Lied* to him.

Bad enough to be taken in by Roland, but to let his goddamn niece sucker him, too? Were those attackers a setup, as well?

But they'd hurt her. And how could she have known where he'd be, to cross his path? Yet she was a banker at the same bank...

Questions whirled in his brain. He got up while Joe was still talking.

"Case?"

"Thanks, Joe," he managed.

"You all right, man?"

"I'll talk to you later." He walked out of Joe's office, disgust and confusion warring with a violent urge to wrap his fingers around her lying throat.

She'd carried her charade off nicely, hadn't she? A blueblood like her would never have wanted a two-bit cowboy like him. How hard had it been to pretend to an attraction? He'd have sworn her response to him was real last night. He drew some small comfort from knowing that maybe she hadn't started out wanting him, but he'd made her crave him, anyhow.

Cold comfort for a charade of monumental proportions.

She'd wipe her lily-white hands clean of him soon enough, and gladly so.

He had news for her. He'd wipe his hands first.

White-hot rage flashed through him again, incinerating every memory of a sweetness he now knew had been just a poor sucker's dream. He didn't understand why she'd done it or what she wanted, and he desperately needed time to think—

But he understood one thing: she'd lied to him. Even if she hadn't known about Roland cheating them earlier, she'd damn sure known before she'd fallen into bed last night and made him feel—

He didn't feel anything. He wouldn't give her the satisfaction. He'd get her the hell out of there and he'd pick up the pieces of—

He slammed his fist against the wheel, then shut down everything but the fury and drove back to the ranch to evict the serpent out of what could never be Paradise now.

But it was all he had.

"Case!" Sammie's delight at his return evaporated the second she got a look at his face.

Case loomed in the doorway. "Wanted to stay around and see if you could finish us off, Ms. St. Claire?"

"What?" Sammie froze.

"*Uncle* Roland didn't take a big enough piece of us, so you came to finish the job?"

Linnie Mae gasped and turned from the sink.

"Was it you who helped him get the loan for us, Ms. Banker from Restoration, so he could take the money and run? Why did you lie to me last night? Poor little Sammie, all alone, no family or friends." Venom dripped from every word.

"We took you in. You ate meals at our table, and you—" He halted. Visibly ground his teeth.

She didn't know this man. Didn't understand what had happened.

She saw no trace of the man who'd made love to her last night. Who'd laughed with her in this kitchen.

"Did you have a good time, playing games with the dumb cowboy? Was it all a setup? What's your endgame? We don't have any money left to take."

Her throat was sandpaper. She tried to move her lips, but words wouldn't come out. She swallowed and tried it again. "Case, it's not what you think—"

"*Don't* say a word—I don't want to hear one lying word from your mouth. I need to figure out what the hell to do now, so I'm leaving before—" He stabbed a finger at her. "You just get the hell out of here. I don't care how you do it or where you go. Count yourself lucky that I don't toss you out bodily—or call the cops. If I could prove that you had anything to do with it, I would. You'd better run, and you'd better run fast, Sammie. I'll be watching for you both, you and that slime you call an uncle, and when I find him, you tell him there will be hell to pay."

"But, Case—"

He turned his back on her, spoke over her. "Linnie Mae, I'm headed to the deer lease to pick up my truck and see if I can scrounge up a load so I can make a run. She'd better be gone before I get back." With that, he slammed the screen door. Seconds later, his pickup roared down the drive.

The silence left behind thrummed with suppressed violence. Linnie Mae looked shell-shocked. Sammie wanted to crawl in a hole, humiliated that she could have played a part in hurting him, hurting any of them. She wanted to beg forgiveness, though she'd done nothing wrong except lie to protect them. She longed to turn back the clock and erase what Roland had done. Linnie Mae's look held such conflict, a deep sympathy and a terrible hurt. Sammie wanted so badly to be one of them again.

But she knew her respite was over.

She was alone once more.

With no idea how to fix any of this.

Chapter Twelve

S ammie couldn't leave.

Not yet. Case's anger was overpowering—but it wasn't unjustified. She had lied to him. That her silence had been out of fear and not ill intent would mean nothing to him at the moment.

But maybe it would, if she dared risk his fury and wait for him to return.

If only she had been able to think fast enough to figure out how to explain as he loomed in that doorway—though accepting that their meeting was pure coincidence wouldn't have been easy, no matter how horribly true it was.

Fate had a cruel, careless hand. Of all the people to come to her rescue...

Needing time and space to think, she saddled the bay mare she'd ridden before. Maybe she'd better consider returning to New Orleans.

A shudder ripped through her at the thought of putting herself back within reach of Gascoigne.

She headed toward the tabletop bluff in the distance, wishing with everything in her to change the past. Her hands shook on the reins as she remembered the look of betrayal on Case's face.

She rode slowly to the top, tears blurring her vision. Why, oh, why, did it have to be Uncle Roland who had cheated

Case? How could he do it to these wonderful, kind people? She thought of Wiley's dear, smiling face. The face of a man so honest he'd never conceive of anyone failing to live up to his expectations of their goodness.

And Linnie Mae, sweet, fierce little woman. She'd taken Sammie to her heart and cared for her as she did everyone else. Sammie couldn't stand to remember her expression as she heard Case's terrible accusations.

Case. Strong, honorable Case, who'd starved for his father's love. What would this do to him? He made himself out to be bad to the bone, but she'd experienced his tenderness. Even when he'd been furious with her, she hadn't been afraid of him. This, though—how would he ever forgive? Would he understand why she'd had to lie? Could he ever separate her from Roland?

Could she?

How could she have been so wrong about her uncle? Had she ever really known him? He'd spoiled her outrageously, probably as much to aggravate Papa as for any other reason. He'd delighted in making her his favorite.

How could she begin to explain this behavior? The Uncle Roland she knew was not an embezzler. He had been a rake, no question about it. He'd taken a perverse pleasure in living below the expectations of society, that too was true. But she'd never known him to be a man to steal from good, kind people like these.

Oh, if only she'd told Case before about Gascoigne and Mr. Whitehead. From the words he'd hurled in anger, she realized that he thought that Uncle Roland was all that she'd been hiding. When he had time to think, she hoped he'd understand that Uncle Roland was not the whole story, once he recalled the abduction attempt. Right now, though, he wasn't being rational about anything, and she couldn't blame him.

He'd suffered a lot in his life, losing his mother at a young age and having a father who abused him. Case had struck off on his own at an age when most boys' biggest worry was who to ask out on a date that weekend. He'd spent years wandering, a rolling stone cut off from all that was dear and familiar, and not once had his father reached out to him. It was difficult for Sammie to understand a family so fragmented. Her own father could be overbearing and difficult, but she'd never had a moment's doubt that he loved her, that her welfare was important to him. She couldn't imagine being Case, having to worry that he and his father would actually harm each other because their relationship was so explosive.

Not that Case was to blame. He'd been a boy then; it was his father who should have known better, should have loved better. Bitter anger rose at the injustice of it all. She wanted to hold the boy Case close to her heart, to make up to him for all he'd had to suffer.

Yet even though he had so little reason to care, he'd come back to take care of the ranch and its inhabitants after his father's death. The scene of his most painful memories must have been the last place he'd wanted to go, but he'd still returned to do the right thing. One thing she'd discovered about Case was that his sense of honor was his guiding light. When the chips were down, you could count on him.

How much would such a man resent being deceived?

And why did it have to be my uncle who cheated him?

In the night Sammie awoke with a start, confused at the sounds she was hearing.

Until she saw the angry orange glow at her bedroom window. Heard the shouts, the chaos.

Fire!

She leaped out of bed, scrambling for the jeans she'd

worn last night. She shoved her feet into her Keds and yanked a t-shirt over her head as she barreled down the stairs.

Outside, voices fought to be heard over the roar of the flames devouring the shed next to the horse barn. Ralph led horses out of the barn, while Wiley's old brown pickup boiled up a cloud of dust, roaring down the road from his house. At the wellhouse, he began rolling out hose so they could fight the fire before it spread.

Sammie ran for the horse barn to help. Trapped horses screamed with fear. Smoke billowed through the opening next to the shed.

Case's roan kicked at his stall door, bellowing loudly. Sammie swallowed hard and headed for him, praying that he would understand she meant to help.

The whites of Comanche's eyes showed, and his nostrils flared. He had never looked more menacing to her, and she quailed at the thought of going closer. Case was the only one who could really control him, but Case wasn't here. She grabbed a rope hanging nearby, grateful it was already knotted into a loop. She threw it over her shoulder as she climbed the slats on the side of his stall.

Frantically she fought to slip it over Comanche's head as his hooves flashed, thundering against the walls. Every strike threatened to topple her from her perch. She crooned to him, not sure that he could hear over the crackling flames and terrified whinnying.

Finally she managed, then leaned down and unlatched the stall door. He lunged for the opening and dragged the stiff rope through her palms as she grappled to hold onto it. Refusing to give in, she launched herself onto his back. She grabbed his mane for balance and laid herself flat on his back, clinging for dear life. Comanche stalled, torn between throwing her off or racing out of the barn.

In the moment of his hesitation, Sammie dug her heels into his side. "Go, boy—Comanche, go!"

He charged for open ground. Terrified he would tangle his legs in the whipping halter rope, she used one hand to try to retrieve it.

"Sammie!" she heard Wiley yell and spotted him running faster than an old man should to help her stop Comanche.

It seemed like forever before she felt the horse slow. "Good boy," she crooned to him. "Good boy. You're okay. We're okay."

At last Comanche stopped, sides heaving, blowing hard, his coat streaked with sweat. The big horse trembled and stamped nervously. Sammie slid to the ground and leaned into him, stroking his neck, trying to impart calm to the terrified animal.

"Damned if I ever thought I'd see such a thing," Wiley said, grabbing the rope. "Never knew anyone could ride that mean sumbitch horse but Case. Don't know that even he could have controlled Comanche in these circumstances, and just look at you, Sammie. Are you all right?"

"I'm…I'm okay." But her voice trembled. "Thank you."

As her heart finally slowed, her mind reverted to what was uppermost: Case. "Wiley…I don't know what to do." She blinked back tears.

"Girly girl, I don't know what happened with Roland, but I don't believe you had any part in it. Case won't either, once he cools off."

"I really didn't. I tried to tell Case before he left, but he wouldn't listen." She tried for a smile. "But there's a fire to fight. Don't you worry about me."

"It's about under control now, and thanks to you, the last of the horses are out of harm's way." Wiley patted her arm awkwardly. "Case will listen to me—or be sorry he didn't," Wiley muttered darkly as he stalked over to put Comanche in a pen well out of danger.

A tired group sat around the table, faces sweaty and soot-stained. It had been a close call. If the barn had burned, if the horses had been trapped... So much could have been lost. Thanks heavens the mother cat had moved her kittens just the day before, tired of all the company.

This was bad, but it could have been much worse.

Sammie and Linnie Mae moved around the kitchen, putting together a snack, pouring glasses of iced tea.

"If you don't mind, make mine coffee," Wiley said. "It's close enough to morning as to make going back to bed hardly worth the effort." He shrugged. "Don't sleep that much, anyway."

Sammie joined him in a cup, certain that she could not possibly rest. Her reaction to the escapade with Comanche was delayed, but now that she had time to think about what she'd done, her insides quivered uncertainly.

"Got to get these children back to bed," Linnie Mae said. "I'll be back to fix breakfast."

"You sleep. I'm not the cook you are, but I could fix it," Sammie offered. "Please."

"Hon, you don't have to do that."

"I want to. Please let me?"

"Let's just say that I'll plan to be here, but if I don't make back before folks get hungry, I'd be much obliged." With a fond smile, she left.

Ralph lingered. "I got a notion what happened."

"You always got a notion, son," Wiley responded. "Some of 'em goldarn foolish." He winked at Sammie.

Sammie couldn't help but smile. Sometimes she thought Wiley and Ralph would be lost without each other to argue with at the drop of a hat.

"You won't think so when I tell you about the kerosene

can I found out back."

"What?" All mischief left Wiley's features. "Where out back?"

"Right where the south shed wall once was."

"You know better than to leave kerosene so close to hay storage."

"I would never do something so stupid."

The two men stared at each other. Wiley spoke first. "You sayin' somebody set that blaze? Who would do that?"

Her breath stalled. Her blood chilled.

"Beats me," Ralph said. "Case would never have left it. I can't imagine who would."

But she could.

They've found me.

She had to leave. She jumped up and busied herself wiping down an already-clean counter, fighting the urge to run out the door.

At last only she and Wiley were left. Sammie looked over at him, lost in his thoughts, a frown on his forehead.

How kind he and Linnie Mae had been to her.

She couldn't leave him puzzling, not when she might have the answer. It was time to share her secrets with someone. Before she left, she wanted Case to know that she was innocent of the crimes he'd charged, even if she couldn't stay to tell him.

"Wiley..." She cleared her throat. "I wish I'd been honest with Case earlier. I had a good reason for lying to him, but it's all gone so wrong, I need to explain—" Her voice cracked with misery.

"What is it?"

She twisted the dishcloth in her hands. "I knew Case had some problems he was trying to solve, but I never had any idea until yesterday that Uncle Roland was involved. I still—I just don't understand how he could have done it. That's not the Uncle Roland I knew, hurting good people like you. Oh, not that he was ever an angel—I'm not saying that." She smiled fondly, remembering. "He's been the black sheep as long as I can remember. Mother loves him dearly, and he's very devoted to her, too. They've had only each other for many years."

Wiley patted her back. "Truth to tell, it still doesn't seem like him to do such a thing, either, honey."

"I appreciate that." Sammie looked up at him, grateful for the support. Summoning the courage to continue. "But that's not why I didn't speak up sooner. I'm in trouble, big trouble, and they told me they'd hurt my family if I talked to anyone, so—" When he didn't respond, she continued. "I swear I never meant to harm any of you."

His level gaze urged her on. She could see no condemnation in it.

"I guess I'd better start at the beginning, only I'm so afraid of what they'll do if they find out. I couldn't bear it if any of you—" She chewed at her lip.

"Why don't you let us worry about that? Seems to me you've been carrying around quite a load all by yourself for long enough. There's not many troubles that can't be improved by sharing them."

She wanted so badly to believe him. She didn't know anymore what to think, what to do next. She'd searched for an answer, but she was no closer than the day she'd left New Orleans, running for her life. These good people had stood by her. They'd been fair and honest when she'd held back too much that was important. If she couldn't have Case's forgiveness, at least she could square things with them.

"My parents are prominent in New Orleans society, and my father is—well, let's just say that he has standards he expects all of us to meet. Don't get me wrong, I love him very much, and I know he loves me, but I haven't always been the easiest child for him to raise. My sisters have always done what he wished. They're both married, one to a doctor and one to a partner in a big law firm. They're seen at the right functions, belong to the right charities…" She uttered a deep sigh, lost in remembrance.

"I didn't openly rebel against Papa, but I just couldn't see myself living that way forever. I had enough of the right parties to last me a lifetime the year I was Queen of Rex." From the blank look on his face, she could tell that Mardi Gras' most famous krewe made little impression on Wiley. Women in her circle would kill to be Queen of Rex, but how empty it seemed now.

"Anyway, I wanted to do something different, but I'm not much good at rebellion. The most revolutionary thing I did was to get a finance degree from Yale and go to work in the bank that was Papa's oldest competitor." She smiled, remembering how hard she'd had to fight over that.

"You see, Papa's chairman of the board of Whitney National Bank, one of the two oldest banks in New Orleans. If I'd been a son, it would have been fine for me to get a degree in finance. But it would *never* have been fine for a child of his, boy or girl, to go to work for Restoration."

She saw his interest spark, surprised that he would be familiar with a bank which was only slightly active in Texas. She thrust the thought away, continuing with her story.

"I was—I am good at banking and finance. I've always been good with numbers, and I did well for myself at the bank. Several weeks ago, I received a strange message from Uncle Roland telling me to look closely at the files on loans generated by Mr. Whitehead, a senior vice-president at Restoration. I wasn't sure why he would ask that, and I felt very uneasy about doing it. I didn't follow up until it was brought to my attention a few days later that an account at the bank belonging to Uncle Roland had been completely cleaned out."

Wiley's eyebrows winged upward. "He has a habit of doing that."

She smiled ruefully. "The bookkeeping department was concerned because a draft on that account had bounced and they couldn't get hold of Uncle Roland. He used to be an officer at Restoration, so they would never think of just notifying him by mail. Uncle Roland was prone to, um, *interesting* investments, so the bank was used to strange comings and goings in that account—but it had never before been cleaned out. The bookkeeper wanted me to know, in case there was something I could do to avoid embarrassing him at the bank. It was an account on which he'd asked me to be an additional signatory long ago." She hesitated. "Things started to get…difficult after that."

Wiley's eyes narrowed. He placed his hand on top of Sammie's tightly clasped knuckles.

The quiet support nearly broke her. Sammie cleared her throat, determined to go on. "When I began to look at Mr. Whitehead's loan files, I noticed several irregularities in them. Documentation was missing, items like appraisals. When I delved deeper, I realized that several of the loans made were clearly much larger than the collateral would warrant." She saw the puzzlement on his face and explained. "That's fraud, if it can be proven. Mr. Whitehead could spend years in jail if it came to light."

Wiley still looked as if he didn't understand why this was significant to Sammie or Roland. She took a deep breath and went on.

"When I looked closer at Uncle Roland's account history, I could see a pattern there. When some of the loans were made, there were corresponding deposits made to his account. I think…I wonder if he was blackmailing Mr. Whitehead. They never liked one another, according to a secretary who's been at the bank forever." She stopped, too miserable to continue.

"Now, Sammie," Wiley soothed. "You don't really know that."

"No, I don't know for sure, but as things turned out, I'm fairly certain."

"What do you mean?"

"I tried to be as discreet as possible in my inquiries, to limit the likelihood of anyone noticing until I could put the pieces together. But I started getting threatening phone calls, telling me that if I didn't leave Whitehead alone, I'd wind up like my no-good uncle. I was concerned, but when I really got scared was when they—" Her throat closed up.

He waited patiently for her to continue, frowning slightly. She took a deep breath.

"One day, I received a package filled with recent photographs of my mother. There was also a note that said she'd suffer if I didn't knock it off. I got a call later, threatening the safety of my entire family if I continued." She looked up anxiously. "I just couldn't take the chance, you see? They told me if I talked to anyone, they'd make sure that my family would pay. I still didn't want to believe them."

"Is that when you left New Orleans?" Wiley questioned.

"No...but things began to happen. My tires were all slashed one day. The phone began to ring in the middle of the night, and my mail appeared to have been opened. But the night I left was when a man—" She couldn't finish.

"You can stop right there. You don't have to relive whatever it was." His jaw hardened, but his gaze remained gentle.

"No, I—I need to tell it all." She shuddered, then straightened her back. "I came home one night, and the apartment didn't feel right somehow. I...it was only a feeling that someone was in there, so I didn't turn on the light, thinking I could get back out and call the police. But he—he pinned me against the wall, and he began to—" She struggled to master her terror as she relived that night.

Wiley shifted. "That's enough."

But she had to finish, so he'd see why she'd kept silent. "Thank God my doorbell rang when it did. He had stripped me—his hands in those horrible surgical gloves were all over me. He said the most sickening things, telling me what he was going to do to me before he killed me." Her arms wrapped tight around her body. She dropped her head and sobbed.

Wiley put his arms around her and rocked her like a child. "Sh-h-h, Sammie…you don't have to talk about it. You're safe here now," he soothed.

She sank against him, then at last drew a ragged breath. "He left through the patio door, but he told me he'd be back. I threw what I could in a suitcase and drove out of New Orleans as fast as I could, heading west. I remembered that the postmark on the letter from Uncle Roland said San Angelo, and I had the idea I might find him there. When Case found me at the truck stop, I already knew I'd been followed and the secondhand car I had traded my Porsche for had broken down. I was sitting in this booth, scared to spend any money for food because I didn't know how long it would have to last, and I had no idea what to do or where to go.

"Case offered to get my car running, but before he could, those men tried to abduct me. He saved me, Wiley, when he didn't have to. He's never been anything but good to me. I'd never hurt him—I didn't know, I swear I didn't know…" Sammie wept for the harm she'd done. For all she'd lost. All they'd lost.

"It's been a long time since I've tanned Case Marshall's hide, but by God, he's got some apologizing to do for not even giving you a chance to explain. When he hears this, he's going to feel like the lowest scum on the planet."

That didn't matter. It would be too late for her.

"Why don't you go on to bed now? The whole world will look better after some sleep. Case won't be back until tomorrow sometime. By then, he'll have calmed down and will be ready to listen," Wiley soothed. "It will all still be here tomorrow. Get some rest."

Wearily, Sammie nodded agreement and started toward

the door.

Then she stopped as she remembered.

"Wiley, what Ralph said about that can—was he right? Could someone have set that fire? I don't know how they'd find me here, but maybe they have. I can't let you all be endangered."

Wiley glanced away, then looked back at her squarely. "Those are just middle-of-the-night thoughts, Sammie. I'm absent-minded as the dickens—I probably left that can there. You go on to sleep and don't worry, hear?"

She wished she could. Wished she didn't know he was saying that for her benefit.

But she knew it was them.

She had to leave.

Chapter Thirteen

Case hadn't gone straight to the deer lease. He'd spent a long day just driving, trying to outrun his thoughts.

Then he'd spent the night trying to drown them when driving hadn't worked. He didn't want to admit how much it hurt to discover that Sammie had felt nothing for him—had instead played him for a fool.

The devil had gotten his due. The seducer had become the seduced.

He'd thought he'd long outgrown his gonads overwhelming his brain, but he could have been eighteen again, for all the sense he'd shown.

Long after the rage fled, a weary acceptance settled in his bones. He should have known she couldn't have wanted a man whose life had been one failure after another.

Bad enough that he'd never been able to earn his father's acceptance. He'd also refused to come home until it was too late, too proud to try one more time.

Then there was the ranch he was so close to losing, the trucking business that was all but gone because he hadn't seen Roland's treachery coming.

Too many failures…and this one the most painful of all. How could he have let himself believe for one minute that someone from Sammie's high-class life would find anything to want in his?

At last he pulled into the deer lease, gearing himself up to call in for another run—

Only his truck had been vandalized, the window smashed and the contents rifled. Who would—

Now that his rage had died down some, he could picture those bastards grabbing Sammie, roughing her up…

If Sammie had been part of Roland fleecing him…

Suddenly he could see more clearly how she'd looked when he'd accused her of being involved with Roland. What had she said?

It's not like you think…

Something was very wrong.

And he didn't have enough pieces of the puzzle to see the big picture.

The memory of her terror rose again. Made him curse her for her silence.

And curse himself for losing his temper and leaving without asking questions.

If she was in trouble, why hadn't she gone to the police? He opened the cab door and surveyed the damage. His gaze went to the compartment where he kept his registration papers.

And his blood ran cold.

If those bastards who tried to hurt Sammie were responsible for this, they knew who she'd been with and where to go next.

No matter that she'd lied to him, he couldn't let them get at her again.

Had to protect all those he loved.

He tried his cell and cursed the lack of coverage in this part of the state. Mostly he liked the remoteness—but not now, not when his gut was churning.

He got back in his pickup and jammed the accelerator to the floor.

Case came bursting in the back door of his house. He'd already called from the road and heard the bad news.

Sammie was gone.

And no one knew where she'd headed.

He'd had miles and miles for his guts to twist, for his heart to ache.

Even murderers got a day in court. Sammie had been the closest thing to happiness he'd ever known, and he hadn't even given her the courtesy of a hearing. He'd ordered her out of his house. Out of his life.

And into what?

There was no mistaking her terror when he no longer had a red film of rage over his eyes. He remembered so many things: how frightened she'd seemed at the truck stop, how reluctantly she'd accepted first his presence and then his help. The way that creep had mauled her, had used his big meaty fists to grope her, to hurt her.

He wanted to hit something, but what most needed hitting was himself.

As he looked around the room, Linnie Mae's eyes were red, the children were crying.

"Where's Ralph?" He felt like an idiot. Who cared where Ralph was? *Where's Sammie?* was what he really wanted to know.

Wiley glared. "Hell, Case, I don't know."

Things were really bad if Wiley was swearing.

Case sat down heavily. Might as well take his lumps. But not for long—he had to get out of here and find Sammie. "Get it over with, Wiley. I know I've been a total ass. Go ahead and lay it on me."

"I can't do near the job you're gonna do on yourself when you hear the whole story, Case. That girl is in danger, big danger, and you just drove her out on her own to face it. I hope you're proud of yourself, you hot-headed son of a—"

Case had never heard him angry like this. "What danger? She was lying about the boyfriend, wasn't she?"

"Boyfriend? What boyfriend?"

"She told me those guys who tried to kidnap her were sent by a jealous boyfriend who wanted to keep her to himself." The look that crossed Wiley's face was all he needed. "Then what's going on?"

Wiley shook his head. "I guess that's what she was talking about when she said she was sorry she'd had to lie to you."

"What do you mean?"

Linnie Mae spoke up. "Case, Sammie's from New Orleans. She worked for a bank there—well, you know that, I guess, after what you said to her."

Case nodded, too weary to speak up.

"She got a strange note from Roland, telling her to look into some loan files at the bank. Yours was one of them, but she never knew that. Your name wasn't the one on it."

Case frowned.

"She noticed irregularities in the files. All of the loans were made for more than the collateral the bank held."

Just like his, only he hadn't known it until the bank came to take back the trucks once Roland split and Case realized that he hadn't been making payments. By then, there'd been no way to catch up.

Linnie Mae continued, "They were all made by the same loan officer at Restoration Bank. About that time, her attention was drawn to an account of Roland's on which Sammie had signatory powers. It had been cleaned out. She discovered Roland had disappeared, leaving word with no one. She started checking around."

Case's attention was riveted on Linnie Mae.

"She came to the conclusion that Roland had been blackmailing the bank officer. She found deposits in his account to coincide with dates on which the loans had been funded. The bank vice-president would make the bogus loan, pocket the surplus, and hand some of it to Roland."

Case whistled. So they hadn't been the only ones Roland had fleeced.

"Sammie's checking around drew some attention, and she started having things happen—tires slashed, mail opened, strange calls. The banker was in league with a mobster named Gascoigne. She got a warning threatening her family if she didn't stop poking around."

Case tensed. "So what happened?"

"What happened, you damn fool," Wiley's tone was thunderous, "was that Sammie was attacked in her own apartment."

A murderous rage grew in Case as Wiley related the details of the attack upon Sammie. Probably the same bastard who pawed her at the truck stop. Case wished he'd killed him, now more than ever. He thought of her nightmare in the truck—how terrified she'd been, how she hadn't wanted to be touched. He recalled the nightmare that had brought him to her bed.

He wanted to grind the bastard's face into a pulp with his fists. Killing was too good for him; he wanted the creep to suffer for a long time.

He welcomed the fury. If he let it take over, he wouldn't have to feel the awful, twisting anguish of knowing that he'd condemned her to more terror by never even giving her a chance to explain.

Bleakness invaded his heart. "That's why she was running when I found her, wasn't it?"

Wiley nodded.

"And it was just coincidence that we ever met."

"That's about the size of it. She had gone to San Angelo looking for him because of a postmark. After that, she was heading for Dallas, thinking she could get lost there—but her car broke down."

"But why, Wiley?" Case barely whispered now. "Why wouldn't she tell me? I asked, over and over. I knew something was wrong. Instead, she lied to me. Why not let me help?"

"They threatened the lives of her family if she told anyone at all. After what they'd done to her, what choice did she have but to believe them? She felt like she had no one to turn to."

"That's why she was afraid of the police—not because she was in it with Roland, but because they'd threatened her family."

Linnie Mae spoke up. "That's why she's gone, too, Case. She's afraid for us, after the fire."

Case's head rose swiftly. "Fire? What fire?"

"The shed behind the barn," Wiley said. "You couldn't smell the ashes when you drove up?"

Case shook his head. "I only had Sammie on my mind. What happened?"

Just then, Ralph walked in the back door. Everyone looked up.

Wiley continued, "You should have seen her, Case. She rescued Comanche from the barn bareback, with only a rope, for God's sake. She faced up to that mean sonofagun lashing out with his hooves. He was trying to kick out his stall door, and she barreled up on top of him and rode him out of the barn, while he tried to throw her all the way. I've never seen anything like it." Wiley shook his head at the memory.

Case couldn't take it all in. "Comanche? She rode Comanche—*bareback*? With only a *rope*?"

Everyone started talking at once, trying to tell the story. Finally, Case waved for silence, his hand raking through his hair.

"She was scared half to death. She didn't stop shaking for half an hour afterwards, but by golly, she brought that mean sumbitch out of there." Wiley's voice rang with pride.

"After we put the fire out and everyone else went to bed was when she told Wiley what had happened," Linnie Mae said. "She wanted you to know that she was innocent." Her voice was tight with accusation.

Damn. He couldn't get past the image of Sammie perched on Comanche's back. Wonder quickly melted away into shame as he remembered what he'd done. He sure didn't deserve her now—

But he was going after her, anyway.

If only he could figure out where she was.

He looked at Wiley. "So she left because she thought it was them?"

Wiley nodded. "Ralph here found a can of kerosene that shouldn't have been there, and she was here when he told me about it. I bet you money that's when she decided to leave. We'd begged her to hang around, told her that you'd cool off and we'd all back her. She'd seemed inclined to do that—until she heard about the can. She didn't say she was leaving, and I thought I'd put her at ease, but I guess I failed."

Case buried his head in his hands, slumped at the table. "If you'd seen those thugs, you'd know why she was afraid. She wouldn't want to endanger any of us. They're scum and vicious. They'd do anything." He exhaled. "She's probably right that they started the fire. I found my truck vandalized. I'm guessing they followed her from the registration information. She's in danger, Wiley, big danger. I wish to God I knew where she was headed."

Despair blanketed the room.

Then Ralph spoke up. "I do."

Everyone stared. He shifted nervously from one foot to the other. "She asked me not to tell, but she had to talk to someone 'cause she needed a ride to town. I don't know why she picked me."

"She always had a soft spot for you, Ralph, when the others were razzing you," Linnie Mae offered.

"Maybe so."

"I don't give a good goddamn why," Case bellowed. He rose, towering over the younger man. "Where the hell is she?"

"She made me promise not to tell, but she didn't tell me about those men. She just said that you were really mad and she had to go. I said I wouldn't tell because she deserves better from you, Case. I wanted to kick your ass myself. But if she's in danger—"

"Ralph, you've got about two seconds."

"I'm not doing this for you." Ralph glared, then sighed. "She's on a bus to New Orleans."

Case's heart sank. She was going back into the belly of the beast.

He shouldn't be surprised. She was feisty, she had spunk—if she'd brave Comanche, she had more courage than most grown men. She'd held onto a dangerous secret, refused to buckle even when her jeopardy was extreme.

He couldn't let her face this alone.

If he had to comb the planet, he'd find her and face it with her. Thank God he knew where she was headed—but New Orleans was a big place.

"Linnie Mae, can you find out the bus schedule and the route for me? Ralph, follow me and tell me everything you can remember about what she intends to do." He headed upstairs to throw some clothes together. No telling how long he might be gone.

He wasn't coming back without her.

Ralph knew very little more, but thank God he'd forced Sammie to tell him where she was going. Case said a silent thanks that Ralph hadn't just let her disappear. The kid had a place here as long as he wanted it.

Case had lived in New Orleans once; he'd call Joe from the road and find out more about Sammie's family. He doubted, from what he'd heard, that she'd go to them, but he had to start somewhere. He'd swallow his pride and call his cousin Quinn, who'd been a detective in Houston, and ask for advice.

Or maybe not. Cops stuck together, and now that he knew she'd been warned not to contact the police…

He'd save that and try it on his own first. He had a good source himself in New Orleans, his club owner friend, Bullhorn Robicheaux. Bullhorn skated just this side of the line and had ties on the other side.

Sammie didn't have anything but what was in her purse, since they'd had to abandon her car. Surely she wouldn't risk letting the mob know she was back by trying to retrieve anything from her place. Maybe she was with a friend. Maybe her family could help him with that.

He thundered down the stairs and headed for his pickup, pausing just long enough to accept the food and coffee Linnie Mae had packed for him and to get the bus information. He knelt before the kids and hugged each one, extracting solemn promises that they'd help out their grandmother, in exchange for his own promise that he'd make sure Sammie was safe. He hoped to God he wasn't lying.

He rose and shook hands with Ralph. "Thank you. You did the right thing, telling me."

Linnie Mae wrapped her arms around him, tears in her eyes. "You stay in touch, you hear? And you stay safe."

"I'll do my best."

Then it was time to face Wiley. The old man who'd been more a father than his own ever was shook his hand, then wrapped him in a hug. "Don't beat yourself up too much over this, boy. I know you would have calmed down and listened to her if she'd been here when you got back. That hot head gets you into trouble, but you didn't bring all this down on Sammie. She was grateful to you for all you'd done, and she was heartsick that someone in her family could have hurt you. She regretted more than anything that she'd made it worse by being too afraid to tell you the truth."

Case's jaw clenched. "And my goddamn hot head sent her back into that hell. No way to duck that, Wiley. But I'm gonna find her—I swear to God I am."

Wiley's eyes misted. He slapped Case on the shoulder. "That little gal is the best thing that ever happened to you, Case Marshall. You'll take care of her, I know you will. Watch your back."

Case nodded, impatient to get on his way. When he backed out the pickup to turn it around, they were all standing on the back porch, waving and wishing him well.

He whispered the first prayer he could remember saying in years.

Please…let me find her.
Let me keep her safe.
And please…give me the chance to seek her forgiveness.

Chapter Fourteen

Clifford "Bullhorn" Brown had a body to match the voice from which his nickname was derived, standing a good six foot eight and almost as wide. Case didn't often feel dwarfed, but he'd never mess with Bullhorn. Even if the man didn't move all that fast, his sheer bulk could still be deadly. Hell, just leaning on a man with that much weight would probably kill him.

Bullhorn needed every bit of that size to compensate for the tender heart lodged inside. As the owner of one of the rowdiest clubs in New Orleans, he was often called upon to restore order. Usually too kind-hearted to act until the situation turned dire, the sheer intimidation of his colossal mahogany frame came in handy when patrons got too boisterous.

His name was apt. No matter how loud the band, Bullhorn could be heard above it—okay, a little exaggeration but not that much. Case had been in the club more than once when everyone turned to hear what Bullhorn was yelling, even though the band was playing full blast.

He was a good friend to have. Once Case got past the towering bulk to the equally large heart inside, he discovered that he could count on Bullhorn for many things: information, entertainment, a good game of chess…and silence.

He needed two of those now.

"Case, *mon ami, viens ici!*" People outside on the street turned to stare as the powerful voice rang out. Case stepped into the dark, dank club and smiled.

"*Quelle problème, boo?* Some *'tite ange* send you home early last night? I didn't think there was a woman alive who'd do dat, but you don' look so good. Come on over here and let ol' Bullhorn buy you a drink."

Another reminder that nothing had been the same since he'd met Sammie. He'd had the best poker face around before he'd met her.

"No, thanks, Bullhorn. Now's not the time for drinks."

"Hoo, boy! It must be serious—the Case Marshall I knew always had time for a drink." Bullhorn smiled broadly.

Case didn't bother to argue. He had once lived hard and played hard, but Bullhorn knew better than anyone that Case never let his drinking get out of hand. Working as Bullhorn's right hand man had meant always being alert and in control.

He smiled wearily. He'd driven straight through, only stopping at bus stops along the way to ask questions and be sure Sammie had stayed on that route. Apparently she had; no one could remember seeing her get off once, except to change buses. They'd hardly noticed her at all, she'd been so quiet. But the driver on the last leg remembered seeing her staring out the window when they stopped. She'd been the last one to leave, and the driver said she'd seemed lost in thought. He remembered her because she'd looked so sad, so fragile. "She had those real good manners, you know? A real lady."

Yeah, he knew, all right.

If only someone had noticed how she left or where she went after that. She seemed to have been swallowed up by the city immediately.

She hadn't taken the bus into downtown but had instead gotten off in Metairie. She was probably afraid of someone she knew seeing her in the downtown area where she would have spent a lot of time when she worked at Restoration

Bank. He'd checked the taxis, but no one could remember her. He'd come up dry on locating her trail.

He'd even made his call to his cousin Quinn, who'd promised to put out feelers, though Quinn acknowledged that his contacts were sorely out of date.

And not once had his cousin made him feel like a jerk for calling out of the blue. He'd been practical and focused—and at the end of their conversation, he'd invited Case for a visit, with or without the woman he was probably curious as hell about.

Case would have to think about that. He'd been without family for so long that the thought of having any would take some adjustment. No question that it was nice, though, not to be painted with his father's sins. Quinn's tone had conveyed honest welcome.

But that was for later. Right now, unless Quinn could come up with a Hail Mary pass, Case could only see a couple of options. He could talk to Sammie's family and see if they'd heard from her—or he could use Bullhorn's network.

He'd rather try Bullhorn first. Sammie's family didn't know him, and Case had a bad feeling about telling anyone who knew her that she was back. He couldn't be sure how extensive was the network of her pursuers.

Bullhorn, on the other hand, could probe his sources and still keep things quiet. He certainly didn't run in the same circles as Sammie, and he had an amazing web of contacts. People swore that if the mayor sneezed, Bullhorn knew it within five minutes.

Back in his office, Bullhorn sat quietly, his gaze never wavering. "A woman. It must be a woman. But not just any woman. I've never seen you like this, *mon ami*. I want to meet this one. Tell me what can I do."

Case looked earnestly into those dark brown eyes peering out from the huge bear of a man.

"I need to find someone, Bullhorn. Someone who doesn't

want to be found. But I can't let anyone know I'm looking for her."

"She married, Case? You avoiding a husband?" He kept his tone light, but the worry bled through.

Case grinned. He hadn't had anything to laugh about in days. Shaking his head, he wished that were all it was.

"No, nothing like that. At least I don't think so. She's in danger, Bullhorn, and I've got to find her to help her. I'm worried about letting anyone else know where she is first."

"What kind of danger?"

"Mob danger, I'm pretty sure."

Bullhorn whistled his surprise. "Bad business, Case. You don't want to mess with dat bunch."

"I know that, but she doesn't have anybody else. This guy, this Gascoigne—I might get her killed just asking questions."

"Etienne Gascoigne? Son, you could get *yourself* killed asking questions."

"Bad guy?"

"The worst. You can't leave this one be? Take a pass and wait for another sweet thing?"

"She's alone, and she's scared."

"And you got that white knight problem." Bullhorn sighed. "So tell me about her. Let's see what ole Bullhorn can do."

Case launched into his story, telling what he knew from Wiley and from his own experience. Bullhorn stopped him and made him describe the two thugs at the truck stop again. When Case did so, Bullhorn whistled again, louder this time.

"*Merde*, Case, dat's Gascoigne's boys, all right, and bad ones. Raymond Boudreaux and Frenchy Pelletier, they both like to hurt people. You crazy, messin' with dat bunch."

He peered closely at Case. "And what you doin' with a high-society girl like her? Seems to me, I remember you callin' them stuck-up bitches that'll tear a man's heart out and feed it to him for supper without breakin' a nail."

Case had the grace to flush. He hadn't had a very high

opinion of the socialites who'd come into the club only wanting to play with a bartender, not fall for one.

"She's different."

"Yeah, I 'spect you right about dat. She'd have to be different to grab hold of a heart as black as yours." His tone was light, but he peered at Case closely. "Oh, yeah, I really want to meet this one, me."

They talked for a few minutes more. Case told him about Roland and asked help to trace him, too. Maybe Roland could clean up this mess—or at least take the heat off Sammie—but first they had to find him. Case would have come to Bullhorn long before if he'd known Roland was from New Orleans.

Bullhorn offered to let Case go to his apartment upstairs and take a nap, but Case couldn't sleep yet. He needed an outlet for the tension in him. He needed to keep moving, keep trying to find her. He told Bullhorn he'd be back later after the club opened, to see what had turned up.

Sammie hadn't slept well in days, not since the night—

She couldn't afford to think about the night Case had made love to her at the ranch. If she spent any more time remembering his devilish grin, those thick-lashed green eyes and their golden lights, that hair that was always curling down on his forehead...

No. Case was the past, and she had a future to figure out.

She still wasn't sure if she was a fool to have come back to New Orleans, or what she thought she could accomplish. She'd had miles and miles to come up with a plan, but every avenue smacked into a brick wall of what she didn't know. What she feared.

She didn't dare contact her family, that was certain. No telling if they were already being watched, but once Gascoigne realized she was gone from the ranch, he'd definitely have her family under surveillance.

The ranch. Wiley and Linnie Mae. All those wonderful, kind people.

Case.

It was a sure road to madness if she didn't stop letting him into her mind. She had a hard enough path ahead of her, eradicating him from her heart.

How had it all happened? Out of all the people in the world, how had her path crossed his? What kind of a cosmic joke was it that a man she'd never have looked at in her former life had become so important to her now?

That wasn't completely true. She'd have looked at Case anywhere—he was far too handsome to ignore. But she'd have seen him only as a bad boy, a hell-raiser out to have a good time, a hot-tempered, sexy devil she'd avoid at all costs.

Not her kind.

But that was in another life.

Though she'd never subscribed to her father's staunch beliefs in the necessity of spending life with what he termed *their kind of people*, she realized now that she hadn't really sought outside her circle for friends—or lovers. She'd never looked down her nose at anyone for his station in life, but she'd spent little time really paying attention to the people who were the salt of the earth. Like Wiley and Linnie Mae. Like Jolene.

She'd let herself be coddled in the cocoon her father had placed around her, rebelling only in going back east to school, taking a job with her father's competition. But even at Yale, where she'd been plunged into a different environment, it had still been a world of privilege, one more cocoon. She'd worked hard at her studies, not dating a lot, but when she had, they'd still been boys not all that different from those she'd chosen in New Orleans.

But very different from Case.

Not a one of them could hold a candle to him. Their lives

of privilege and comfort had made them soft. Oh, yes, they might be ambitious, sharp-edged in their desire to get ahead. But for all his posturing as the devil incarnate, Case was a knight in shining armor. He might tell the world to go to hell, but when it counted, he was there.

How unwelcome her troubles must have been when he'd had so many more of his own than he had told her, yet he'd still placed himself in danger to protect her. He'd spent his sorely-needed money on her. He'd shared his tenderness and his passion with her. Remembering him, the soul-deep, bone-melting flame that he was, how he could draw longings out of her that she didn't even know she possessed... She shivered, feeling the desire once again sluicing through her veins.

If only she hadn't been so nervous about Roland. If only she hadn't been afraid to confide in Case.

If only she'd made love with him one more time.

She couldn't believe that she, Samantha St. Claire, was making such a statement. Passion had never been a part of her life. She'd appreciated beautiful music, great art, good conversation, fine food...all at a safe remove. Now she understood that she'd sleepwalked through most of her life.

She'd been so determined not to let love make her a slave that she'd become a slave to that vow. She'd let the meaning of life pass her right by—until a rogue named Case Marshall had made restraint and reason impossible.

She'd never experienced the intensity of feelings that she'd known since she met Case. Even through the terror, the strain, the anguish of running for her life, she'd never felt more alive. His courage, his strength, his compassion—all these had brought blessed water to an arid life. The bright flame of desire he'd sparked within her...she'd never known anything like it. She couldn't imagine living without it again...but she'd have to learn.

Because Case was gone. She'd never see him again. Never spot that mischief in his eyes, never hear his honeyed words tempting her, never feel those strong, clever fingers tease her, make her tingle, make her burn. Never feel that body she loved...

Love. Plain and simple, there it was. Sammie loved Case. Dear God.

But she couldn't have him. Oh, she believed Wiley—Case would have cooled down. He would have listened.

But would he ever have trusted her again?

He'd been hurt too badly, too many times. She'd gladly give the rest of her life to making it up to him. She'd share all she knew of the business world to help him rebuild. She'd share her money. She'd certainly give her body. But would he want her heart?

And would he give her his?

She couldn't think about him anymore. Couldn't let herself remember all the people she'd come to care for at the ranch. Couldn't allow herself to feel how she'd give up everything to be able to go back there, make a life there.

Because she was poison. Unless she could find a solution to her problems here, she had no future. She'd only endanger anyone who was near her. So she had to harden her heart, hone her mind, figure a way out.

Or she'd have to run forever.

She couldn't see her family. She couldn't contact Case. But she'd thought of someone she could see, someone not really connected to her who might let her stay for a while as she puzzled this through.

Jerry Benson was her mechanic. He'd worked on her Porsche, the rebellion-red dream car she'd fallen in love with and then had to leave behind.

He'd become her friend. He was a redhead, medium build and kind blue eyes. He had come to New Orleans from St.

Louis to visit a cousin and never left. His world and his background couldn't have been more different from hers, but that hadn't seemed to matter to either. When she had her car in the shop, she'd linger just to chat.

They didn't see one another often. For a while, after he'd worked up his nerve to ask her out and she'd demurred, their relationship had been strained. She'd even thought about finding another mechanic, but Jerry had gone back to laughing and teasing again, and everything had been all right.

She wasn't sure why she hadn't gone out with him. He was nice enough, and she liked his wit. He wasn't gorgeous like Case, but he was nice-looking and anyway, looks had never meant much to Sammie. She wasn't a snob; she didn't care that he was her mechanic. He was good to her, he was kind and thoughtful, he was strong in his own way.

But he felt like a brother.

"You seem upset. What's the matter, my friend?" Jerry asked as they stood next to the cash register in the office of his garage.

"Jerry, I—" She glanced away. "The thing is...I need a place to stay."

His eyebrows rose. "No problem. I've got room. You know I live over the garage, but you're always welcome."

No questions asked. He was a good friend, not even questioning why she didn't go to her own apartment.

"But—" She heaved a big sigh. "You should know I'm in trouble and there might be danger."

"What kind of trouble?"

She rubbed her arms, chilled despite the July heat. "It's a long story."

"I'm not going anywhere. Come on up and have a glass of iced tea. I can hear the bell up there, and anyway, I don't think anyone's going to do much this afternoon. It's too hot to move."

That was the truth. Until she'd gone to Yale, she'd never fully realized how incredibly hot and humid New Orleans could be. Tourists always complained about it, but she'd been there all her life and hadn't given it a second thought until she'd lived somewhere else.

"Need to get anything from your car?"

How could she tell the man who'd found it for her and cared for it like it was his baby that had been left behind in Houston? "It's...not here."

"How'd you get here?"

She squirmed a little before meeting his gaze. "It's gone, Jerry—I had to sell it."

"Why on earth would you do that?"

She filled him in on Gascoigne, stressing that he, too, could be in danger if he gave her a haven. She skimmed over her time at the ranch, not realizing that the longing in her tone gave her away when she talked about Case, though she mentioned him only briefly.

"So where are your clothes?"

"What I have here is it." She found herself amused by his horror as he took in her Wranglers and her pink Keds, the outfit she'd donned as a memento of her time at the ranch.

"What about all those designer suits and stuff?"

"They're still in my apartment, I guess."

"Okay, let's head on over there—" He subsided. "Oh. You can't really go over there, can you? It might be watched."

That he caught the implications of her situation so quickly was a relief.

"Well, that's okay. Make me a list of what you want and I'll go get it."

"No! You can't be seen going over there, either. You could get hurt."

"Nonsense. You don't even know that they're watching your apartment."

"You have no idea what they're capable of." She couldn't help a shudder. "Please don't take any chances." She clasped his arm.

"You're all I have left."

Chapter Fifteen

It was too early for Bullhorn's joint to be jumping, so Case hoped they would have time to talk. He'd been wandering New Orleans all afternoon, trying to imagine where Sammie might hide out. He'd looked through crowds in the Quarter, stared in streetcar windows, walked the streets of the business district. A hundred times he'd thought it might be her he was seeing, only to have his heart plummet at the realization that the woman moved wrong, or her hair wasn't right, or the voice didn't have that chocolaty tone that drove him wild.

He had her parents' address on Prytania Street. He'd driven by there, dismayed to see just exactly how wealthy her background was. The house was Greek Revival, with columns and broad galleries and manicured grounds. How could he ever hope to take her back to the ranch, knowing she'd grown up in this kind of luxury? What did he have to offer her? A broken-down ranch? An old pickup? A black heart and a hot temper?

He wasn't husband material.

After seeing the house, he'd walked around for an hour, struggling with the urge to chuck it all and head back.

But no way could he leave her alone. Even though he now knew just how unsuitable he was, he still had to help her. No leaving until she was safe.

Whatever that meant. There was still too much he didn't

know.

He had found out her apartment address, and he'd driven by to see where she lived now, almost hoping she'd gone back there, despite his fear of the danger to her. He'd been surprised; it wasn't opulent like her family home, a garden apartment near the lakeshore, pretty but not ostentatious.

But she wasn't there, either. The place had an abandoned air about it.

Tired and discouraged, Case hoped Bullhorn had good news. He walked into the club where music played over the intercom as patrons converged, waiting for tonight's act to show. It was already noisy, and the pool tables near the bar were occupied. Seeing no sign of Bullhorn, he walked to the bar and ordered a beer. He was leaning against the bar, deep in thought, when a pair of arms slid around his waist.

He whirled and saw Dolly Wadsworth grinning from ear to ear. He grinned back. "Hey, girl—what are you doing here?"

"We're playing here tonight. Didn't Bullhorn tell you?"

"Not a word. How are you doing?" Case was a little uneasy, remembering how much she'd riled Sammie, but Dolly and he went way back, and it was nice to see a familiar face.

"I'm fine, but why are you in town? Where's your little darlin', lover man?"

Case stiffened. "She's not here."

"Well, gorgeous, I can see that for myself. Left her back on the ranch?"

His voice tight, he responded, "Drop it, Dolly."

She stroked one finger up his shirtfront, circling around his nipple and looking at him through fluttering lashes. "You're wound tighter than a spring. Want to get together after the show and…relax? We've always been good together, Case."

He recoiled at her touch. Dolly was a skilled lover, and he'd had his share of good times in her bed, but her caress was not the one he wanted.

Dolly dropped her hand. "You've got it bad, don't you? She's really gotten to you."

"It's not like that—"

Her laugh was clear and bitter. "The hell it's not. You forget—I've watched you together. You never looked at me that way."

Case shifted uneasily.

"Oh, hell, what do I care? You're the best goddamn man I ever knew, and nobody makes love like you. But I'm not a one-man woman, and we both know it. If anybody could have made me one, it was you, you big jerk. She's damn lucky. I hope she knows it."

I doubt it. Case sagged against the bar. *Not after what I did.*

Dolly laid a hand on his arm, eyes searching his. "Can I help?"

He shook his head. "No, but thanks. Seriously. This is something I have to figure out on my own."

"I hate to see you so miserable." She caught a signal from the stage, where the crew was finishing the sound check. "I've got to go, but if you decide you'd like a little comfort, I could help you forget for a while. I wouldn't take seconds from anyone else, but you're not just anyone."

Case felt worse than ever. "You're a good woman—better than I deserve, probably. But I can't."

She stood on tip-toes to give him a light kiss. "Well, I'll be here, sugar, if you change your mind." With a toss of her hair, she walked away, hips swaying in that slow, seductive rhythm that drew every eye in the room.

Case followed her with his gaze. He was probably a damn fool for turning her down. He had no future with Sammie, he knew that—

But she was the only woman he wanted.

Inside Bullhorn's office, which was decorated in Early Bordello Meets Psychedelic, Case recalled many a night he'd spent in here after closing, shooting the breeze. Bullhorn treated his staff more like family, and tonight was no exception. When Case arrived, the man had been counseling a devastated waitress who'd just found out she was pregnant with her third child after letting her good-for-nothing husband into her bed one last time before she booted him for good.

This scene was nothing uncommon. At one time or another, everyone who worked for Bullhorn had come to him for help. He'd been married years before, but his wife and baby had died in childbirth, and he'd never stopped mourning the loss. Case supposed Bullhorn had decided it was easier to build a family out of the odds and ends of his employees after that.

Case had been the exception, and he didn't like asking for favors now, but he needed this one. As his search for Sammie continued to bear no fruit, his sense of urgency dogged him. She faced mountainous odds, and she was alone. He had to find her before Gascoigne knew she was here, right in his back yard.

The look Bullhorn turned on him was not encouraging. "These things take time, but I am not discouraged. About you, however, I am concerned. Your *'tite ange* has apparently jeopardized a very cozy arrangement, and she will be dealt with—at whatever price. I ask you again, Case, is she worth it?"

Case jammed a lid on his temper. "Bullhorn, you've been a good friend and I owe you, but I don't want to hear any more of that crap. I'm not leaving until I find her. Now what about Roland?"

Bullhorn shook his head and sighed. "There we have

news that's a bit more encouraging. Roland, he has been spotted in town recently. He isn't staying with his sister or at the hotel he usually frequents when he is in town, but he has been seen. He, too, is in grave danger. This is not his first offense, but he has tended to gravitate toward minor con games in the past, so those in power did not worry about him. Until he got too greedy with his little blackmail scheme, they paid him little mind. But now they, too, search for him. I hope to have more information tomorrow. Come see me at breakfast."

"All right." He had no real choice, but damn, he wanted a piece of Roland. The man had gotten Sammie into this nightmare. How could anyone do that to family?

But she was his first priority. Every hour that passed increased the danger that Gascoigne would find her first.

He paced the small office. Bullhorn stopped him with a hand on his arm. "Why don't you go to my apartment and rest?"

"No!" Case barked. He exhaled in a gust. "Sorry. I know you're trying to help, but I can't relax. She's out there somewhere, all alone and in grave danger, and I can't rest until I find her."

"You'll be no good to her if you're too exhausted to think straight." Bullhorn's tone was gentle.

"I know that, but how the hell can I rest now?" He wheeled to leave. "I've got to go. I'll be back."

"Why don't you stay and watch Dolly? You love her act."

"I'm in no mood to be entertained." Case stopped at the door and turned. "I'll be back."

In the wee hours of the night Case sat in his pickup outside Sammie's apartment. He'd decided to stake it out and see if he could tell whether it was being watched. If not, he thought he might see about breaking in himself. Maybe he could find some clue in there that would tell him where else to look for her. It might not be the best plan, but he was running out of options until he turned up more information. Quinn had called him and passed along much the same as he'd learned from Bullhorn: Gascoigne was dangerous and his organization was on high alert. Quinn urged him once again to turn this over to the cops, but Bullhorn had added his own caution to the warning Sammie had relayed to Wiley. Gascoigne had cops in his pocket, and Quinn reluctantly agreed that he had no way to know which ones. Alerting them carried with it too much danger for Sammie and her family.

"I can come down there, Case. Be another pair of eyes. I've done my share of undercover work, which is more than you can say."

Case had been floored by the offer. "I can't ask you to put yourself in harm's way. You have a family that needs you."

"I have family walking around New Orleans, flirting with danger. You should have backup. You have no business playing detective."

Case had been simultaneously stunned to hear himself termed family so matter-of-factly while also more than a little ticked off by what he knew was only the truth. "I've spent my time on the wrong side of the tracks. I can handle myself."

Quinn heaved a sigh. "If I'd ever had any doubts, I'd know you were a Marshall by the thickness of your skull."

Case chuckled. "Thank you—seriously. After what my old man did…"

"You're not Black Jack. And that's water under the bridge. Family is important to Josh and me—deal with it."

The gruff tone was more heartwarming than sympathy ever could be. Case had gotten off the phone after promising to check in and to let Quinn know if he'd changed his mind about asking for backup.

Damn. Family. Who knew having nosy relatives could feel so good?

So here he sat, waiting for dawn's light. He was considering going to see Sammie's family, but he certainly couldn't do that at this time of night. He wasn't due to see Bullhorn until breakfast—and breakfast around there meant noon. He had time to kill.

The night was sultry; cicadas hummed all around. He almost wished he smoked; it would give him something to do as he waited, scanning the area. So far he'd seen no sign of surveillance, but he figured he'd better take it slow. It would be better to try his attempt to get into her apartment later. He had no tools, but he had an idea Bullhorn could help him out with that. Bullhorn's friends were many and varied.

His eyelids began to droop. He couldn't actually remember the last time he'd slept a whole night. He closed his eyes, telling himself it was just for a moment.

Sammie's eyes flared with the heat of longing. He could smell her skin, the faint twist of cinnamon curling through him, stirring his blood. Her whiskey hair fell in waves, tantalizing him with its silky touch as she stroked it across his belly. He strained toward her, but she danced just out of his reach. He groaned, and his head fell back as he remembered his promise to remain still, arms at his sides, prohibited by his vow to refrain from seizing her until she gave him rein. She was torturing him with honey-sweet kisses, drawing her beguiling aura around him with velvet tongue, sharp teeth, dancing fingers.

He knew he could overpower her and take what he craved. There were moments when he was sorely tempted. But he'd promised, the way lovers do. It was her game, one they'd both enjoy, he knew—if he didn't explode first. He trembled with the force of his need, fingers curled into fists, trying to resist the urge to yank her down upon him, to roll her over and plunge into her, deep and fast. He wanted her...oh, God, how he wanted her...

He turned his head toward her, perhaps to beg for mercy—and saw the terror in hers as she was grabbed from behind, her throat squeezed by the ham-fisted Frenchy Pelletier. As her mouth opened to scream, Case tried to rise, held down by an invisible force, rendering him helpless to save her—

Case jerked awake, heart pounding.

Dreaming. He'd only been dreaming. He looked around.

Movement off to his left grabbed his attention. He sat up straighter, barely daring to breathe. His window was open in deference to the heat—he couldn't run the a/c and risk alerting anyone to his presence.

Just then, the shadow moved again. It was a man of medium height, slipping stealthily between cars, with what looked to be a small toolbox in one hand. As he disappeared around a corner of the building, headed toward the courtyard, Case slipped out of his truck through the open window.

He stayed low, gliding from shadow to shadow, careful not to brush against anything. As he rounded the corner, he saw the man nearing Sammie's apartment. His heart skipped a beat. At last. Maybe he'd been given a break.

He wished he'd gotten a gun from Bullhorn. Who was this guy?

In moments, he saw the door open and the figure dart inside. No lights came on. No surprise there.

He saw tiny, sporadic flashes as whoever it was kept the use of a flashlight minimal. He waited and watched. In a few minutes, the figure emerged with a suitcase and some items of clothing thrown over his arm.

Clothes?

Yes. Whoever this was had to know Sammie. Friend or foe, he'd lead Case right to her, surely.

Case raced back to his pickup and once again climbed

through the window to keep the dome light off. The guy was getting into a van up the street. Case left his lights off and began to follow, careful to leave space between them. Only when they were off the quiet street and back on a main thoroughfare did he turn on his headlights. He kept pace with the other driver, his heart racing as he focused on not losing his first real hope of finding her.

They headed toward Old Metairie, and Case cursed as he lost sight of the van. He changed lanes as a truck ahead moved over, and he spotted the van again. After making several turns, the van pulled into the parking lot of an automotive repair shop, and the driver emerged. He headed toward the back of the building and up a staircase, disappearing inside the door at the top of the steps.

Was she being held there? Had they finally caught her? Why would she be in a commercial district, above a mechanic's shop? But if she was a prisoner, why would they care if she had fresh clothing?

Case decided he'd better wait. The sun was coming up, and he'd be too visible. Though he was half-crazy with the need to charge in and look for her, instead he drove past and circled the block, looking for a place to park where he would be inconspicuous. When he found it, he settled in to wait. He still had until noon before he had to meet Bullhorn.

As morning dawned, he saw the door open at the top of the stairs. His breath left him in a whoosh as he recognized Sammie coming down the stairs, smiling at the man he'd seen last night.

She didn't look like his Sammie anymore. Her hair, that beautiful whiskey-brown hair he loved to touch, was caught up in an elegant twist, not a strand out of place. Her suit was creamy white, the double-breasted jacket topped with pearls at her throat. The knee-length straight skirt accentuated her slimness. She carried other clothing over one arm, a filmy garment of some sort, with sandals dangling from her hand.

This cool elegance was as foreign to the laughing woman in pink Keds as anyone could possibly be.

When she looked at her companion and kissed his cheek, Case's blood boiled. When she touched the man's arm lightly and bestowed a teasing grin, Case wanted to pound the guy's face into a pulp. He ached to go to her. His heart stirred, just seeing her.

But what did he really know about her life? Had she made love with him when she was involved with this guy?

Stop that. You didn't trust her before and look what happened.

As the two neared the van, Sammie turned in Case's direction for a moment. He could see her face clearly; the haunted look she wore was unmistakable. So who was this guy? She was obviously there of her own free will, but if so, why didn't she look happier?

As the van pulled out of the parking lot, Case started his pickup. When it refused to catch, he tried again and, like a total rookie, managed to flood the engine.

He pounded the steering wheel. Hell. He looked down the street. She was gone. He laid his forehead on the steering wheel, trying not to succumb to despair. He raised his head and rubbed his eyes with the heels of his hand. He'd wait a while, until he had to meet Bullhorn. Maybe she'd come back.

He spotted a cafe down the street. He didn't want to leave, but he needed the men's room and coffee. He left his pickup and set out on foot, hoping like hell that he wouldn't miss anything important.

When he entered the cafe, he felt right at home. The clientele must work in the shops scattered along this street. No one was talking much, just drinking coffee and reading the paper. Instead of taking a booth, he went to the counter and ordered coffee to go, excusing himself to use the restroom while they fixed his cup. When he returned, he joked with the waitress, then asked if she knew any good mechanics. She pointed down the street and told him that the guy's name was

Jerry Benson. A quiet guy who did a good business, he lived over his shop. Case thanked her and left quickly, wary of being gone too long.

He'd finally found her.

He'd stick around—this guy was his only connection to her.

He was not going to lose her again.

Chapter Sixteen

Sammie couldn't stop jumping at shadows, even though she'd taken every precaution she could think of. Two unique outfits, as different as night and day, even altering her behavior when she'd been with Jerry at each car rental place. At the first, she'd been stern and forbidding, a tough-as-nails career woman. They'd rented a black Lexus, paying for it with cash and using Jerry's ID.

At the second, she'd been a kitten, coy and dependent, leaning on Jerry and playing cutesy games. She'd let her hair down and teased it into a wild mane to complete the gypsy image of dangling bracelets and flowing, filmy skirt. They'd used his ID again, something she worried over but had no other option. She hadn't the faintest idea how to go about getting fake IDs. Jerry had wanted her to let him take care of the whole thing, but it was bad enough that she'd had to borrow money from him when she had plenty sitting in a bank account she didn't dare touch.

They'd taken the additional precaution of using one agency in New Orleans and the second in Metairie. They'd parked the Lexus at a nearby mall. When they'd picked up the second car, a nondescript white Ford sedan, she'd urged Jerry to go back to work.

He hadn't wanted to leave her, but she'd finally persuaded him by pointing out the importance of letting nothing appear out of the ordinary at his place. It wasn't unusual for him to close up for short periods to pick up parts, but he would really raise some eyebrows if he closed for the day in the middle of the week. Only the argument that he'd be protecting her hideaway succeeded in convincing him to go on back.

What she intended to do now was possibly foolish, but she was in the Taurus with heavily tinted windows, she told herself. If she drove carefully and quickly past, she could try to figure out if her parents' home was being watched. She didn't dwell on how badly she wanted some contact with her old life.

As she drove down Second Street, snippets of her childhood trailed through her mind. Under the huge old trees, she'd skipped and played with her sisters. She'd played hopscotch and jacks with Mary Louise Bremond, her oldest friend. That young Samantha could never have imagined being afraid to enter this neighborhood, much less haunted by the possibility that she would find herself a danger to her family.

When she turned onto Prytania, she had to force herself to objectively view her surroundings. Few cars were ever parked out on the street, and she saw none that looked out of place. As she neared her family's home, her longings intensified. What she wouldn't give to drive under the porte cochère and run inside to find her father's strong arms, her mother's love. Her eyes swam with tears when she spotted a form in the gazebo across the expanse of lawn. Her mother. It had to be her—she'd know that slight form anywhere.

The sharp edge of guilt, coated with the bitterness of desperation, pierced her soul. She couldn't endanger her mother—it was madness to be so near. For just a moment, she let herself think of the comfort of laying her head in her mother's lap as she had done as a child in that very gazebo. The scents of her mother's beloved garden filled her nostrils, the soft, cool touch of her hands on Sammie's hair soothed and calmed her. No trouble had ever seemed too unmanageable, no obstacle insurmountable when viewed from the cradle of her mother's love.

Sammie wished, in that instant, that she'd never grown up, never realized how fragile her mother was. It was she who was the stronger, she who had to protect her mother now. Sammie made herself drive off, however much she longed to have it all go away.

As she pulled to a stop at the next corner, she reached across the seat to fumble in her purse for a tissue. Her thoughts raced ahead to her next move, when her eye was caught by a car turning onto Prytania from First Street. She wasn't sure what had snared her attention—perhaps some animal instinct for danger older than rational thought. She slumped in her seat barely in time to spot a head that looked frighteningly as if it belonged to the man named Frenchy who'd grabbed her at the truck stop.

Heart pounding, she stared into the rearview mirror. Maybe she was wrong.

But if she wasn't... Pulse racing, she started the car and tried desperately to calm herself, fighting the instinct to floor the accelerator in her haste to escape. Memories of his hands groping her, imprisoning her, his harsh voice cursing her and taunting her with what he'd like to do to her—

Stop it. Think what to do next.

She calmed herself by recalling Case racing across the parking lot, the answer to her prayers.

But Case wasn't here. He would never be with her again. She had to fight this battle and beat the odds alone.

Still, the thought of Case gave her strength. She remembered most his courage, his solid confidence, his teasing tenderness...the thrill of his touch. Nothing had seemed to be insurmountable when he was near. She yearned to lean against him just once more, to replenish her own strength in the bottomless well of his. He'd said she had courage; she'd have to prove him right.

She tried not to think about how she'd ridiculed love for making a person weak. Loving Case made her feel stronger.

As she sped away from the neighborhood, she decided that her next step would be to return to the mall where the other car was parked. There was a movie complex there, she recalled. She'd sit in a darkened theater and figure the move after that.

After the repair shop had gone an hour past the regular opening time without a sign of the man or Sammie returning, Case considered whether he should leave and head on back to meet Bullhorn later that morning. His gut told him to wait.

A sudden inspiration led him to start the engine again—a smooth process when he wasn't acting like a madman. He pulled up in front of the garage and lifted the hood. He used the time to do a general inspection of all the systems. His impulse was soon rewarded when the man he'd seen with Sammie earlier pulled into the drive and headed in his direction.

"Can I help you?"

"You work here?" Case looked out from under the hood to meet the steady gaze of the redheaded man who'd touched Sammie so lovingly. He throttled back on the urge to grind the man's face into the pavement.

"Yeah, this is my place. Jerry Benson," he said, offering a handshake. "What seems to be the problem?"

"Luther…Luther Cantrell," Case offered. Until he understood more about what Sammie was doing here, he'd remain disguised. "I'm not sure. This pickup has gotten me down many a mile, but it's running rough this morning."

"Want me to take a look at it?" Jerry's gaze was friendly, if a little cautious.

"Not exactly your usual type of vehicle, is it?" Case challenged.

"No, but that's only because the luxury cars pay better. My clientele is accustomed to sparing no expense. My background is in hot rods, farm equipment, you name it." He grinned, the easy smile making Case clench his jaw. Damn it, he refused to like this son-of-a-gun who laid hands on *his* Sammie. The irony of the thought was not lost on him. He'd be lucky if his Sammie didn't spit in his eye when she saw him, after the way he'd treated her.

Jerry misinterpreted the twist of Case's mouth. "Hey, it's no skin off my nose if you don't want me to help. I've got more business than I can handle."

"Sorry—no offense intended." He'd just had a brilliant idea, a possible way to be allowed to wait around to see if Sammie showed up. His tone apologetic, he continued, "It's just that—well, I'm not too flush right now. I can do my own work, but I don't have enough tools with me. I wonder if I could trade with you, free labor in exchange for using your tools later on."

Jerry's eyes narrowed. "What kind of experience do you have?"

"A lot like yours. A little bit of everything from big rigs to farm equipment to passenger cars."

"Any foreign car experience?"

"Not a lot, but I could stick to the simple stuff and leave the fancy work to you." Case forced himself not to push.

Jerry studied him. "Well, it's no lie that I could use the help. I guess it's worth a shot. Just don't do anything you have the slightest doubt about, okay? We'll talk our way through each vehicle first."

Case tamped down his jubilation and merely nodded. "Sounds good to me. Let's get to work."

They worked in a companionable silence for the next few

hours. Jerry brought lunch from down the street, saying that it was the least he could do for the free labor. Most of the time, the only sound in the garage not work-related was the radio Jerry kept tuned to a talk show. Case didn't mind; it relieved him of the need to talk and risk revealing anything about himself to this man he was coming to like against his will. He was grateful for the distraction. He wasn't sure how much longer he could stand not knowing what was happening with Sammie. Having work to do helped the time pass.

Jerry came over to the MG on which Case was adjusting the timing. "Luther?"

Case took a split-second to respond and hoped Jerry hadn't noticed. "Yeah?"

"I've got to make a run for parts. I'll just lock up and put up the sign so no one will bother you while I'm gone."

Pleased that Jerry would trust him enough to leave him with the tools, Case nodded and returned to work.

Sammie left the mall, dressed once again in the suit, her gypsy outfit in the shopping bag she clutched in one hand. The suit was now accessorized with a big hat and sunglasses, obscuring her face. She'd decided to drive by her apartment and see if she could spot any surveillance there.

As she neared her apartment building, her heartbeat picked up. She tried to stay calm, to be observant and not dwell on the fact that this was her home. What mattered now was ending this nightmare so she could go back to her life and not harm those she loved. After what had happened up those stairs, she was less sure that the apartment would ever feel like home again, but that was something to figure out later— assuming she ever got the chance.

She didn't see anything out of the ordinary at first. Then

she spotted a large sedan parked across the street and down the block a bit. Was it the one from the truck stop? She couldn't be sure—too much had happened that night.

As she neared it, however, she heard a roaring in her ears as her heartbeat sped up. Black dots danced at the corners of her vision.

Breathe. Calm down.

It was the same car. Oh, God. The bitter taste of terror scalded the back of her throat. Did they know she was here, or was it merely a precaution? She pressed a hand to her heart, willing it to slow down. She drove past, staring straight ahead, afraid she'd alert some animal sense in them if she didn't get herself under control. She forced herself to drive at a moderate speed, knuckles white on the steering wheel as she fought to keep a grip on her sanity, to rein in her terror.

She had her answer. She had no choice but to go forward—no going back to her old life now. She had to find a solution.

Or remain a fugitive forever.

"Hey, Luther, it's time to knock off for the day. If you want to use my tools to work on your truck now, it's fine with me," Jerry offered. "Want to grab a bite before you do?"

"Thanks, but if you're willing to leave me here, I'll just go ahead and get to work. I've got a friend I need to see, and I'd better head out pretty soon," Case responded. He'd managed a quick call earlier to leave Bullhorn a message not to expect him.

"If you were going to take off with my tools, you could have done that before now. Want me to lock up?"

"No, it's pretty hot. Leave the door open, if you don't mind. I'll punch in the lock before I leave, if you're not back."

"Okay. Go out the back way and lock this deadbolt from inside. I'll be back in a couple of hours." Jerry paused until Case looked up. "Thanks. You do good work. Don't suppose you're looking for a job?"

"Sorry, no."

"Well, if you change your mind, you've got one here."

Case held out his hand. "Thanks. I'll remember that. Much obliged." Jerry shook hands with him, then turned to leave.

Sammie's exhaustion was as much mental as physical. Fear and confusion had taken their toll. This nightmare seemed to go on and on, an endless cycle of terror. As she ascended the stairs to Jerry's apartment, she wondered if she should insist on relocating. Maybe he could loan her the money for a motel room somewhere. She could be endangering him, too, without knowing it. She'd tried to be careful, but she was a novice at this. How did she know if she'd been careful enough? She thought about the precautions Case had taken. His instincts had given her a margin of safety, a time of respite. Time was what she needed most, time to figure out what to do to end this nightmare. She wished, yet again, that Case were here. Together they could solve this, she just knew.

Case. Her thoughts always came back to him. She had to stop thinking about him, had to stop longing for him. He wanted nothing to do with her, and she had to get over him.

"Jerry?" she called out, knowing already from the feel of the apartment that he wasn't here. She'd look downstairs in the garage, where a faint light spilled onto the drive.

The side door to the garage was open. She passed through the darkness, gravitating toward the light. "Jerry? Are you here?"

She neared the pickup hood from which the light was coming, and all her senses prickled. When she came around to the side, she lurched to a halt, stunned by the shock of what she saw.

Case. He was here. Here, before her very eyes, surely a vision conjured from her longings. Her legs nearly collapsed.

Their gazes met as he lay barely under the truck, the air snapping with the shock. The longing.

She couldn't speak. Couldn't comprehend that he could truly be here. He'd told her to get away from him. She knew she was supposed to forget him, yet here he was, a dream come to life. She fought the urge to run to him, to sob in relief at seeing him. She ached to go nearer.

The night closed in around them, and the sounds from outside crept in slowly, birds settling down to rest, cicadas humming in the sultry summer night. The garage was humid and dark, the trouble light hanging near him the only illumination, shadowing his sable mane and angular beauty. He shouldn't be here. She shouldn't want him to stay. He was dangerous to her resolve, and she was a danger to him. She should turn and run away—far, far away.

But she wanted him…oh, how she wanted him here.

The sight of him stole her every last thought. He lay there, his long, muscular legs spread, giving her a clear impression of the bulge that had worn his jeans almost white. Lay there with that powerful chest and the ropes of muscles layering the arms she wished with all her heart she could feel around her once more.

Temptation. A dark angel. Carnality as pure as sin.

And maybe the love of her life.

She wanted this man. Craved to forget everything else and lose herself in the fog of desire filling the space between them. To crawl into his arms and never leave.

No one had ever pulled at her like this, had ever wrapped himself around her without coming close enough even to touch. He was six feet away, for heaven's sake, and her heart was pounding.

Case tried to look unmoved. He was anything but. Unsure of his welcome, he was nonetheless certain of how much he wanted her. She was the lightning rod for all of his longings, amplifying them back at him in pulses so powerful that all he could do was to lie there, his body pounded by wave after wave of hunger for her.

Sammie watched him rise slowly, wiping the grease from his hands with a rag. His hair was tousled, hanging low over his right eye, shadowing the arresting brightness of those green eyes. As he moved toward her, she took a step back, unnerved by the draw he exerted, afraid to believe there was a chance for them. She was stopped by the hard wooden edge of a workbench, and she placed one hand on his chest as if for protection.

It was a bad move. Her hand came to rest on his warm flesh at the point where his shirt opened onto a hard ridge of muscle. Desire arced between them, shock thrilling through her. Her fingers flexed into the crisp hairs, nails lightly grazing his flesh. Hot wells of need threatened to boil over.

She looked up quickly as his head bent to her, his gaze fixed on her lips with a burning intensity. She used her tongue to quench the searing sensation. His eyes smoldered at the sight.

Case was trapped as surely as a deer in headlights. He could no more move away from her than leap to the moon. There might be a thousand reasons for them to be apart, but right now none of them meant a damn. He wanted her so badly his gut ached, but he didn't want to frighten her. Needing to touch, he reached out with one finger, marking her cheek with one lazy, smooth streak of grease.

She felt both branded and caressed.

Sammie grasped that hand with her free one and slowly, very slowly, her eyes never leaving his, streaked his mark across her bare skin just above her bodice, then moved his large, warm hand to cup her breast.

Mesmerized by her bold move, desire crackled through him like a bolt of lightning. Her fingers slid up to his shoulder and drew him closer until he dipped his head and drank of those lips that were driving him mad. A slow, soft moan rose from deep within her as he got a taste of what he'd been craving.

Barely able to breathe, he cruised his lips down her pale throat.

She gasped softly, and her nipple tightened beneath his palm.

He used his teeth lightly to secure his claim, his tongue soothing the soft bite. As she melted into his arms, he drew her close, but nothing seemed close enough. Every rational thought drowned out by the buzz of desire, he lifted her to the workbench, shoving the tools aside with one sweep of his arm.

She hardly reacted to the noise, so filled were her senses with his presence. This was a wildfire burning out of control, and nothing short of the Second Coming was going to stop it. She surrendered, catching herself on her elbows, head falling back as that wild, scorching mouth of his worked its magic down her body.

His hands slid up under her slim, tailored skirt, giving him a view at last of what he'd remembered at least a thousand times in his dreams. He wanted to fall to his knees before her, a poster girl lying there, every man's fantasy, sensuality incarnate, draped in sexy disarray on the workbench. If this was a dream, he prayed never to awaken.

He started at the end of those long, tempting legs, removing her heels and cradling one slender foot in his large hand. As he bent to kiss her instep, she sighed.

His tongue made its way up her curvy calf to lick around to the back of her knee.

Sammie moaned. She felt exposed, wanton…tantalized. Her arousal deepened when his hands eased her legs apart and caressed the inner curves of her thighs. By the time he tortured his way upward, his heated breath whispering across the dark curls, she was panting and shifting restlessly. He slid her panties off and she plowed her fingers into his thick dark hair, grasping and flexing in frenzied bliss as the magic of his tongue sent her soaring.

She couldn't stand any more, mad with need for him to fill the aching void he'd left when he'd sent her away. She levered up and grabbed for his belt buckle, both of them fumbling with the fastening. He returned his hands to her body, his face tight, visibly struggling for patience to wait for her to free him. He stripped off her suit jacket and caressed her breasts, working at the tiny buttons of the severe blouse covering those curves.

When they succeeded, both breathed sighs of relief. His gaze met hers in shared amusement at the sound.

The amusement didn't last long. His eyes darkened, and hers closed as he buried his fingers in her hair. He drew her to him for a slow, scorching kiss.

"Oh, Case…." Just like that, she was rising again, her body gathering to fly once more.

"Look at me." His voice was rough. Hungry.

When she did, he made them one.

She gasped. He groaned, standing stock-still and drinking in the solace after the long, painful separation.

Then urgency gripped them once more and they began to move, this time together in a dance as old as time, as primal as the beat of blood rushing through veins. Higher and higher they climbed together, yearning unrelenting and intense.

Breathing hard, thrusting deep, Case couldn't get close enough.

Finally, he picked her up, still full and aching within her, and settled on the high stool next to the workbench. She perched her feet on the rungs at the sides, rocking sinuously above him as his strength supported both of them. She wrapped her arms tightly about his neck, lowering her head to mate with his mouth while her hot, sweet warmth stroked him with agonizing pleasure. Her hair formed a dark, glowing curtain around them, little whimpers escaping her throat. Case groaned from somewhere deep in his soul, and the firestorm consumed them.

Moments later, as her head rested on his broad shoulder and nerve endings screamed from the power of their release, the phone in the office rang.

"There's no way in hell I'm answering that, even if I thought it was for me." Case's voice was still husky, still raw.

Her lips quirked up in a lazy smile, and his tilted in answer. They were still for a moment, reveling in the closeness. He closed his eyes to savor the moment before reality could split them apart again.

Words had been the enemy. He wasn't ready for them yet.

Chapter Seventeen

S ammie tensed and slid off his lap. Picked up her panties
and put them on with her back to him. Then she retrieved
her blouse and worked on the buttons, face still averted.

Case moved to stand behind her, one hand hovering just
above her shoulder. He was suddenly unsure of his right to
touch her, painfully aware of how he'd wronged her.

*Hell with that. She's welcome to yell at me all she wants, but I'm
going nowhere.*

He turned her into his arms, willing her to stay…to give
him a chance. Shaken by the power of what they'd experienced, he knew, without a doubt, that Sammie was all he'd
ever wanted in a woman. She was the mate of his dreams—
fiery magic, tender warmth, intelligence and strength. A man
could spend all his days with her and never truly understand
her, certainly never tire of her. She soothed his troubled soul
in a way he'd never let himself wish for.

He stroked her hair as he wrestled with his need to pos-
sess her, to shield her. He was afraid of words—he'd hurt her
too much with words—but somehow he needed to make her
know that he was sorry, more sorry than he could ever find
words to say. He'd spend the rest of his life trying to make it
up to her for not giving her a chance to explain.

When she leaned into his caress, he took his first real
breath and cradled her head against his shoulder, wrapping

her more securely against him. He laid his cheek on her hair and exhaled a sigh of pure pleasure. For just these few moments before they had to face the pain of the past and the uncertainties of the future, this was…perfection.

"Sammie, I'm sorry."

"Case, I'm sorry."

They spoke in unison, then halted, waiting for the other.

Case pressed on. "I'd say *Ladies first*, but you don't owe me an apology. I let my cursed temper get out of hand and never even gave you a chance to explain. I deserve your anger. Anything you say against me won't compare to what I've said about myself. I thought Linnie Mae was going to take me over her knee. She was spitting mad that I behaved like such an ass. I don't have a good excuse—I just felt so betrayed."

"You had every right. I should have trusted you and told you the truth, but—"

He didn't let her finish. "After what you've been through, how could you know who to trust?"

"I knew I could trust you. You've—oh, Case, you've done so much for me. I don't want you involved in this. You need to go back."

"Like hell I will. I'm already involved. There's no way I'm leaving you to face this alone. Don't waste your breath trying to discourage me. I've scoured New Orleans looking for you."

Sammie's gaze met his, emotion brimming over. Long moments ticked away before she answered. "I wish I could say I didn't need your help. I couldn't bear it if you were hurt."

Elation surged, washing away nights of anguish and despair, endless hours in which he'd cursed himself for his cruelty and thoughtlessness.

He swept her up in his arms, burying his face against her throat. Slowly he began to turn in a circle with her, and her back arched in bliss, her glorious locks draping over his arm.

Just then, Jerry walked in. "Samantha, Luther, what the hell—?"

Sammie jackknifed in surprise, and Case nearly dropped her.

"Luther? Who's Luther?" she asked.

Jerry pointed a finger at Case. Her eyes narrowed.

Case shrugged. "Hey, I didn't know why you were here or who he was. It seemed best…"

Jerry scowled. "Then just who the hell are you? And what are you doing with Samantha?"

Case set her down but didn't let go. He grimaced, realizing that he still hadn't finished buttoning his jeans. He extended his hand, trying to make the best of things. "Case Marshall, Jerry. No offense intended."

Jerry regarded his hand like a venomous snake. He shot Sammie a piercing glance, and Case could tell he knew exactly what they'd been doing.

Then Jerry sighed and accepted the handshake with a disapproving glare at Sammie. "Looks like you've decided not to take my advice."

Sammie blushed.

Case's arm slid around her waist, drawing her closer to stake his claim. *Too bad, dude. You're a nice guy, but she's mine.*

Jerry's face tightened, but he said nothing.

Sammie touched his arm, and Jerry flinched.

He studied the floor briefly, then sighed and looked at both of them. "Well, it looks like we've got some catching up to do. Come on upstairs. I think we all need a drink. I know I do."

As he turned to lead the way, Case arched one eyebrow at Sammie. "Some history there?"

"I'll explain later."

She started to follow, but Case held her back, threading his fingers through her hair and stealing one more long, scorching kiss. "We've got a lot of catching up to do, too, beautiful."

She responded hungrily. When the brushfire threatened to spread out of reach, Case drew back reluctantly, hanging his head and struggling for control. "I wish to hell we were home right now."

"Me, too."

He blew out a breath. "Guess we'd better go on up. Not fair to rub it in." He slung one arm around her shoulders and led her out of the garage.

Sammie wove her fingers through his as they draped over her shoulder, a soft, tender smile playing over her face as she leaned into his side.

They ordered pizza delivery. Sammie was surprised to discover that she was ravenous. For the first time since she'd left the ranch, the thought of food was enticing. As she sat next to Case on Jerry's couch, she began to have hope that she might come to a good end, after all. No question that there was danger ahead, no doubt that she had hardship in store. But somehow, Case's very presence gave her a glimmer of optimism. She was no longer alone.

Jerry brought Sammie a glass of Chardonnay and Case a beer.

"Sammie." Case's voice was low, his tone grim. "Catch me up on what's been happening."

The day's discoveries came bounding back, and dread took over. How could she have gotten so lost in Case when there was so much danger around them? "I saw them—the men from the truck stop. The one who hurt me."

"Where?" His jaw tightened.

She began to relate the events of the day, unable to sit still as she told him about spotting Frenchy. She paused before a picture on the wall across the room, staring sightlessly, remembered horrors swamping her brain.

When Case touched her, she practically jumped out of her

skin.

"Hey, I'm sorry. I didn't mean to scare you." He gathered her close.

For a moment, she let herself surrender to the comfort of his nearness.

"I'm not letting you get hurt, not ever again."

She tipped her face up to his. "I'm not so afraid, now that you're here."

"You've been damn brave through everything, but I won't kid you. I'd rather you were tucked far away, somewhere safe."

"But it's not going to go away. If they really did find me at the ranch, they can track me anywhere."

Sorrow chased over his face.

"They did, didn't they? How?"

"They broke into my truck. I'm pretty sure they got the address of the ranch from my registration papers."

"Then they did set the fire. Oh, Case, how can you worry about my forgiveness when I should be begging it from you? I can't stand knowing that innocent people have been endangered and it's all my fault. I should have kept running—I wish you'd never stopped to help me. I've been nothing but trouble since the day you met me."

Case grasped her by the shoulders. "None of this is your fault. This is all so foreign to anything you've ever experienced, yet you keep dredging up the courage to search for a way out. Don't you dare wish I'd never stopped to help—if I'd never met you, I'd still be wondering why I bothered to get up every day."

His eyes blazed with emotion so fierce that it yanked her out of her misery. Knowing that he cared gave her a reason to fight for a future. It roused the stubborn spirit that was both blessing and curse to her.

"So what do we do now?"

His jaw flexed. His gaze went steely.

"Now, we find Roland."

Chapter Eighteen

When they entered Bullhorn's club, Sammie tensed as she recognized Dolly's voice.

Case cast her a rueful grin and guided her around the edge of the crowded room. As they neared the right side of the stage, Dolly crossed to them, still singing.

Sammie stared defiantly right back at her.

Dolly's gaze was not that of a woman who wished her well.

When Case drew her on, she glanced up to find him glaring at Dolly.

"Don't worry about her," Case spoke, his breath a tickle upon her ear. "She's nothing to me, I swear."

"I'm not worried. I want to rip her hair out by the roots."

Case burst out laughing. "Wow, the society girl has a mean streak." He gently played one long finger across her cheek, then drew her onward.

She hazarded one last glance at Dolly, only to see an expression of such wistfulness that sympathy stirred. How could she blame any woman for wanting him?

Then they reached a door that swung open as they approached. Inside was the most enormous black man Sammie had ever seen. His attire was eye-popping—a diamond stickpin sparkled from the lapel of an iridescent green/gold suit. His tie was a colorful silk scarf, and one earlobe gleamed with the brilliance of another impressive diamond. His fingers flashed as he moved, each bearing a ring of some sort, even his thumbs.

But what she found most arresting was his eyes. Large and liquid dark, they shone with curiosity and welcome. The moment she laid eyes on him, she felt that she'd found a friend.

"So the prodigal finally returns."

When he spoke, she nearly jumped out of her skin.

Bullhorn laughed, and Case chuckled. "His bark is worse than his bite," he assured her. "It's been some time since I've seen him draw blood."

Bullhorn muted his voice and beckoned. "Come here, *chère*, don't be listenin' to no reprobate like Case here. This one, he don't know nuthin' 'bout how to behave around a lady." He rose and graciously offered his arm to escort her to the chair beside his. When she was settled, he offered her refreshments, but she declined politely.

He turned to Case. "I knew she would be special, but you never told me she was a real lady. This one, *mon ami*, you treat like crystal, you hear me? Bullhorn hear dat you bring one tear to her eye, and we gonna see 'bout drawin' blood." His voice carried a serious note beneath the teasing.

"You don't have to remind me how precious she is." His gaze on her was hot yet tender.

Bullhorn resumed his seat beside her, drawing her hand from her lap and cradling it between his huge paws. The top hand patted her gently as if to reassure her.

"What have you found?" Case asked.

"Well, *'tite ange*," Bullhorn addressed himself to Sammie first, *"Ton oncle, il n'est pas comme toi, bien sûr."* His tone was almost apologetic.

It was Sammie's turn to pat Bullhorn's hand in commiseration. *"C'est vrai, M'sieur Bullhorn."* Her tone was as mournful as his. If she'd ever doubted that her uncle was not like her, recent events had cured that misperception.

They continued to converse in French, Bullhorn bemoaning the deplorable lack of civility in a conversation she could easily imagine having with her mother. The very notion of the two of them in one room made her want to giggle.

Case cleared his throat loudly. "If you're finished with your little tea party, Bullhorn, I'd like to get back to the subject. You said you had information on Roland. What did you find out?"

Bullhorn sighed extravagantly. Turning to Sammie, he rolled his eyes in annoyance. "*Pardon, ma jolie fille.* I must now deal with this barbarian who accompanied you. We will continue our little chat later, *oui?*"

Sammie smothered a grin.

When Bullhorn spoke again, however, the somber tone sobered her. "He's still in town. We don't yet know where he's staying, but one of my contacts spotted him yesterday near the home of an old bookie friend."

As Case and Bullhorn kicked around possibilities for finding out where her uncle might be located. Sammie's mind began to wander. Case's presence had relaxed her enough to realize just how keyed up she'd been, and fatigue hit her like a wall of water dragging her under.

Maybe splashing some water on her face would help her perk up. "I'll be right back. Which way is the ladies' room?"

Bullhorn offered to escort her, but Case was beside her in an instant.

"I'll go with you."

She smiled. "I don't think you'd be allowed."

"I meant—" He reddened. "You know what I meant."

She placed a hand on his arm. "I'll be fine. Back in a minute, okay?"

"You look so damn tired. We'll finish up before you get back, then I'll take you home."

Home. Only the ranch felt like home now. Shaking off the

maudlin thought, she smiled, then winked at Bullhorn. "Sounds like a plan to me."

Splashing water didn't help her energy much, but it did cool her off a bit. The club was packed, and the air conditioning strained to do the impossible. Dolly had the crowd whipped into a frenzy. Sweating, gyrating bodies were everywhere. As Sammie edged along the wall on the opposite side of the club from Bullhorn's office, she had all she could do to squeeze through the scant extra space, dodging bodies swaying and shaking in celebration.

A man stood in her way, and she searched for a way around his bulk.

Something hard and metallic dug into her ribs.

A voice she'd hoped never to hear again slithered into her brain. "Well, *putain*, you and me, we got some unfinished business."

For the second time that day, she stared into the terrifying face of Frenchy Pelletier.

He grabbed her arm and pressed the gun into her waist, then dragged it upward until it stabbed into the tender underside of one breast.

She tried to jerk away, but the dancers behind her mashed her up against him. She glanced around frantically, hoping someone would notice what was happening.

"Don't even think about it. No one can hear you. Dolly, she's making them lose their minds right now. You just turn around and start walking toward that door in the corner."

Sammie stood her ground, daring him to create a scene. She had to buy time for Case to find her or for someone else to notice her distress.

If she let him take her out of here, she was lost.

He jammed her against the wall and ground his pelvis into hers, his face contorted in rage. "If you want trouble, bitch, just try to get cute. I don't have a schedule for showing up with you—you and me, we could have some fun before we get there."

Sour acid rose. The thought of being alone with him…

She'd already had proof that he'd welcome any chance to maul or terrorize her. Her thoughts raced as she searched frantically for a way out.

A cocktail waitress was finishing with the table behind him. She had to get the woman's attention.

She forced her body to relax. When his tension eased, she shoved him as hard as she could into the back of the waitress. The woman whirled around, spitting mad, drawing the attention of the people in the immediate vicinity.

Sammie scrambled away, but he rebounded toward her, murder in his eyes. The press of bodies gave her no room to maneuver.

He lashed out with the pistol, catching her on the side of the head. As she fought to keep her feet, she screamed "Get Case!", hoping that the waitress knew who Case was. Frenchy grabbed her arm and dragged her out the door into the night.

Raymond Boudreaux waited there.

She didn't go easily, fighting Frenchy with everything she had.

Finally he hauled back and punched her so hard that she collapsed like a sack of potatoes, ears ringing, barely able to hear him yell, "Block that door, Ray—let's get the hell out of here!"

The atmosphere in Bullhorn's apartment was grim. It had become a command headquarters of sorts, as Bullhorn reached out to every contact he had to try to find where Gascoigne's men might have taken Sammie.

There was no doubt that's who had done it. The waitress's description of Frenchy was unmistakable.

Why the hell hadn't anyone stopped him? She'd been in the middle of a goddamn crowd.

Why had he let her out of his sight for one second?

Inside Case rumbled a volcano ready to spew out dangerous poisons, wreaking havoc on everything in its path. He paced the rooms, crazed to be out there looking for her, even though he'd agreed that it would be a pointless search, with nothing to go on.

Frenchy could have taken her anywhere. Gascoigne owned extensive properties that would provide hundreds of places to go to ground.

Case had no choice but to stay until they could get a break.

But being this helpless was killing him.

"Goddamn it!" Case's fist smashed into the paneling, startling the other occupants of the room. "Where in the hell could she be, Bullhorn?" Agony hoarsened his voice. Fear for her crushed his heart in a fist.

"Case…" Dolly started toward him, hand out for comfort.

"Are you happy now? You got what you wanted—Sammie's not here anymore." He knew he was wrong to savage her, but he was desperate to strike out, a madman in his frustration and fear. She recoiled as though slapped, then turned and left the room.

"Don't do this, *mon ami*. She's not who you want to hurt," Bullhorn chided.

Case sagged to the sofa, rubbing his hands over his face, then raking them through his hair.

Then he jumped right back up and resumed pacing.

Lashing out like a wounded animal didn't help anyone.

These were his friends. They deserved better.

But his stomach turned at the thought of what might be happening to Sammie.

Bullhorn approached, the only person in the room big enough to dare to get close. He laid a hand on Case's shoulder, holding him firmly in place. "Case—"

The telephone rang. One of his aides answered, speaking quietly, then listening intently.

Not a soul in the room moved. Case barely breathed.

The aide hung up and spoke to Bullhorn. "Nothing on her yet, but we've found Roland Bracewell."

"Where is the little sonofabitch?" Case demanded.

Bullhorn's man looked over at his boss for permission. When Bullhorn nodded, he told Case the name of the motel.

Case turned to go. Bullhorn reached for him as he passed, but Case shook him off, his eyes shooting a warning that he would not be forestalled.

"I won't try to stop you, Case, but take one of my guys with you. Let him drive—it will save you time and perhaps you will get there alive."

Case nodded tightly. Clasped his friend's shoulder. "Thank you. I'll check in."

"I will keep looking for *la 'tite ange, mon ami*. We'll find her." The promise in his voice was firm.

Case had little faith in anything right now, certainly not Fate's tender mercies.

But Fate had seen nothing like the revenge he would wreak if anything happened to Sammie.

Chapter Nineteen

The door to Room 122 of the Bayou Motel exploded inward, the wood splintering at the hinges from the force of Case's body hurtling against it.

"Case!" Roland sounded delighted to see him

His expression turned uncertain as Case's towering anger registered.

He began backing across the room as Case advanced. "Now, see here, my boy, let's don't be hasty now. I don't have your money right now, but I'll get more for you, just as I did before." He scrambled into the corner, brandishing an umbrella as his only weapon.

Case snarled and snatched the umbrella from him, launching it across the room, hearing it crack against the wall. He enjoyed the fright on Roland's face. "To hell with the money, Roland."

"Oh, you don't need it? Well, I daresay, that's very helpful, but I don't quite see—"

Case grabbed the once-dapper little man, fighting the urge to punch his lights out. Too bad he needed the little prick's help. "Oh, I intend to get every penny back, Roland, don't you ever doubt it. But right now, I want Sammie."

Roland's eyes bugged out. "Sammie?" He blinked, as if Case had spoken another language. "Do you mean Samantha? My Samantha?"

"No, Roland, *my* Samantha," Case growled. "The woman you left to face the music when you turned tail and ran. The woman who's been running for her life, thanks to you." His fingers wrapped around Roland's throat as he fought the urge to squeeze the life out of him. "The woman Frenchy Pelletier beat up and carried away a few hours ago, you lousy piece of shit."

All the color drained from Roland's face as he visibly recoiled in horror. "Frenchy?" he croaked weakly. "Gascoigne has Samantha?"

Case released him and Roland slid to the floor, gasping. "Get dressed," Case snapped. His fists clenched and unclenched as he paced the floor. The moment he had Sammie back safe, he would grind this weasel into the dirt.

Roland scuttled over and removed another of his white planter's suits from a hanger, the awkward gait a reminder that Roland was not a young man.

Case hardened his heart against any sympathy. This was the man who'd caused all of Sammie's troubles. Because of him, whatever his reasons for doing what he had, she was in grave danger. Every second might mean the difference between life and death for her.

But he had a plan. Roland was going to be bait to flush out Gascoigne. It was fitting; he'd made Sammie bait—now he'd get to do the honors.

"Case, you must believe me, I never intended...I love that girl as though she were my own. I would never—"

"Don't say you'd never—you did this to her, Roland. You dragged her into a nightmare. You turned her life into a living hell. What in the devil were you thinking? How could you involve her?" Barely suppressed fury vibrated in his voice.

Roland flinched from the violence in his tone. "But I don't understand—why didn't she turn the matter over to the authorities? Let the police and the bank examiners handle it?" His confusion seemed genuine.

"Because Gascoigne's brutes told her they'd harm her family if she told anyone. They backed it up with some pretty nasty demonstrations on Sammie."

Roland sucked in his breath but didn't speak.

Case continued. "Nice little things like beating her, trying to abduct her. And then there was Frenchy Pelletier, stripping her and almost raping her in her own apartment." Case didn't even try to restrain the menace he felt for this weasel.

Roland squeezed his eyes closed, a struggle on his face. "Please believe me, Case. I would never—*never*—have put her in this position if I'd known. Tell me what I can do to help."

Roland's shaken composure began to breach Case's anger, convincing him that perhaps the man really had not anticipated the carnage he'd wrought.

"You, my man, are going to serve as bait."

Roland blinked rapidly, but surprisingly drew himself up to face the task. "Very well. Where do we begin?"

Case felt pretty stupid, dressed up like a delivery man for his visit to the St. Claires' opulent home. Knowing that Sammie had spotted surveillance on this street, however, he didn't dare show up undisguised. He wasn't happy about the delay, but Roland was insistent that he must speak with his sister before meeting with Gascoigne.

It wasn't like Case had a lot of options. Bullhorn still had no word on Sammie's whereabouts, so he'd seized upon Case's idea of using Roland as bait. If they couldn't find Gascoigne, they'd make sure he had reason to want to find them. Bullhorn had set about sending word through all his channels that Roland wanted to meet with Gascoigne to hand over files he had that Gascoigne wanted.

Now they were playing a waiting game, one Case hoped

like hell would end soon. Every time he thought about what Frenchy and Ray might be doing to Sammie...

He was strung taut as a bow from his sense of foreboding, half-crazed with his need to get to her. He'd seen what these creeps were willing to do to her, and her earlier escapes would only make them more determined to make her pay.

The door finally opened.

"Yes?" A maid stood there, polite in her unconcern. His disguise must work.

"I have a package for Mrs. St. Claire. She has to sign for it in person."

"Can't someone else sign?"

"No. Only Mrs. St. Claire. I can't leave it with anyone else."

Her mouth a prim line, at last the woman nodded. She closed the door in his face and left to fetch her employer.

The quick view he'd had of the enormous black-and-white marble entry and the elegant, curving staircase made it easy to picture Sammie gliding down in a ballgown, heart-breakingly beautiful.

He could also imagine her descending those same steps as a bride, and he was painfully aware of what he would be asking her to give up to come live with him. Parents who lived like this wouldn't be happy.

The door re-opened, and he got a glimpse of Sammie as she might look years from now. The woman before him was beautiful, too, though she lacked Sammie's vibrancy. This woman looked fragile enough to break. Linnie Mae smaller, but her eternal vitality, her roots in the harsh land, made her a mighty oak compared to the will-o-the-wisp standing before him.

"You asked for me?" He hadn't realized he was staring, until the woman's quizzical look forced him back to the present.

"Mrs. St. Claire?"

She nodded.

"Sorry to bother you, ma'am, but this package must be signed for by you personally, and my instructions are to have you open it in my presence."

"I don't know…" She looked nervously around her.

Of course a woman of her age and station would not be comfortable letting a delivery man into her home, but he had to be with her when she opened the package and read Roland's message. "You could open it out here, if you wish, where we could be in plain sight, Mrs. St. Claire."

She hesitated and studied him. "I suppose it will be all right for you to come in," she offered. "The servants will be nearby."

"Thank you, ma'am." Case removed his cap and stepped inside, enjoying the cool comfort of the entry.

Sammie's mother took the package to the large library table on which stood a tall crystal vase filled with fresh flowers. Her back was to him, but he could see her reflection in the huge mirror mounted over the table. As she read the address, her brow wrinkled slightly. Her skin was smooth as a girl's, he noticed. Her figure was trim, her bearing graceful. The silver in her hair and the slightly blurred lines of her face were the only clues that she was not Sammie's age.

From a drawer in the front of the table, she took a silver letter opener to slit open the package. She opened the single sheet of paper nestled inside, written in Roland's own hand, and gasped. Her eyes met his in the mirror. She turned. "Who are you, young man? And where is my daughter?"

Case stepped toward her, halting as she retreated in fear. He'd intended to comfort her, he realized, but she didn't know him from Adam.

"Mrs. St. Claire, I'd give a lot to know that myself. Your daughter is in serious danger, and I'm doing everything I can to find her, but I need your help." When she didn't speak, he continued. "I don't know how much you know about what your brother has done, but I'll leave that to him to explain. Suffice it to say that she is in the hands of people who won't blink at killing her."

The woman gasped, and he rushed to assure her. "I am not going to let it come to that, but I need Roland's cooperation in order to rescue her, and he's insisted upon talking with you first."

"We have to call the police."

"We can't," he said grimly. "They have issued very credible warnings against your lives that sent her running away in the first place. They've found her, and I have to get to her immediately. I need you to trust me, Mrs. St. Claire. Your daughter means everything to me. I'd give my life to save her."

"We should speak with my husband."

"There is no time. Don't you dare slow me down, Mrs. St. Claire. Her life is at stake, and I won't hesitate to mow down anyone in my path." He exhaled. "I don't want to scare you, but I can't emphasize enough what a dangerous situation she's in."

She frowned. "How do you know Samantha?"

"It's a long story, and time is critical. Whether or not Sammie wants me in her life isn't nearly as important as making sure that she's alive to make that decision."

Mrs. St. Claire looked deep into his eyes before she spoke again. "I cannot leave with you, Mr.—?"

"Marshall, ma'am, Case Marshall. But you have to—"

She interrupted. "I cannot leave with you because my husband would find out, and I cannot be sure what he might do. I have no wish to endanger him, nor do I want anything to happen to my daughter. I will meet you at the entrance to the Audubon Zoo in thirty minutes." She began to walk away.

"Fifteen minutes. Please."

She revolved, one patrician brow lifted.

"We have to hurry. He's already had her at his mercy for

hours."

Her expression was stricken. "You are sure this will work?"

Hell, no, he wasn't. But to her he only said simply and from the heart, "I'll get your daughter back, Mrs. St. Claire. I won't consider any other outcome, whatever it costs me."

She studied his face, then nodded. "I'll tell my driver to hurry."

Not knowing was the worst part, Sammie decided. That must be how prisoners of war were broken down, by the gnawing uncertainty of having no idea if help was coming—or if anyone even cared.

Case will come, she chastised herself. *He will come for me.*

If she could just hold on.

If only Frenchy would stay away.

She shuddered and curled into the back seat upholstery, desperate to make herself less noticeable. Bound and blindfolded, she was still dizzy from the blows she had taken when she'd fought to keep him from dragging her out of the club.

The car stopped. The back door opened.

He ran those meaty hands up her legs. Grabbed her ankles and pulled her legs apart, dragging her body toward his.

It was all she could do to remain limp while he groped at her and muttered crude curses in bastard French.

"Frenchy! There will be hell to pay if you don't get her inside this second."

He yanked her the rest of the way out, then threw her over his shoulder and stomped his way inside. The feel of his thick hands on the backs of her legs, of her breasts mashed into his back, was so disgusting she couldn't repress a shudder.

She forced herself to relax immediately—but too late.

"*Putain*, you will pay for the trouble you have caused me." With relish, he recited a litany of details.

She wouldn't let herself listen. Could not afford to, not if she hoped to get out of here.

Despite everything, she did. She had no idea how, and she was hopelessly outmatched—

But she still clung to the hope that Case would come after her. In the meantime, she would stay alert for any opportunity to escape.

Wherever they were, someone must have stored chemical fertilizers here in the past. There was a strong, acrid smell which reminded her of chemicals the gardeners used on her parents' lawn.

Frenchy tossed her on a cot. She landed on top of a scratchy blanket.

His hot, fetid breath washed over her face. He shoved one hand between her legs.

Sickness rose. *Oh please oh please…*

The other voice called out. "Frenchy, goddamn it, where the hell are you?"

One more ham-handed squeeze. "I will be back, bitch. Count on it."

Oh, God. The thought of being alone with him…

She heard a door close and she thought she might be alone, but she wasn't taking any chances. She kept herself completely still, using one deep breath after another to calm herself. To will away the urge to be sick.

The only thing that helped was thinking of Case.

But it seemed a sacrilege to recall their lovemaking while in this place of horror. She felt so exposed. So terribly vulnerable. The memory of Frenchy's filthy hands touching where Case had caressed her so tenderly—

No. She couldn't think of them so close together.

She would concentrate on her bindings. He'd probably

done them this way to make her feel more helpless, but the way he'd bound her arms behind, forcing her breasts to thrust out, might work to her advantage if she could arch her back enough to bring her ankles near. Her wrists were bound too tightly for her to work at them with her fingers, but perhaps, before she lost all feeling in her fingers, she could pick at the ankle restraints.

She blessed her yoga classes for her flexibility, but it was all she could do not to cry out when one hamstring cramped up. She straightened her legs again and focused on relaxing the muscle. She would try again, slowly arching and breathing into the movement as though she were in class. She would also listen for any hints about where she was and what was happening.

And she would pray for rescue. She wouldn't give up on rescuing herself, but she was out of her league and she knew it.

Please, Case, please hurry.

Chapter Twenty

C ase's patience was strained to the breaking point, waiting
for Gascoigne to make contact. Every minute that
passed, every half-hour, seemed an eternity—one in which
Sammie could be lost to him forever.

He smashed one fist into the other hand, drawing the attention of everyone else in the room.

Sammie's mother flinched, and he lowered his eyes in
silent apology. She didn't deserve his anger; she was nervous
enough.

When he'd brought her back, she and Roland had em-
braced warmly, Roland rocking her from side to side. He drew
his sister away to a corner of Bullhorn's living room to speak
with her, and Case had to admire the way she'd taken the
details about Sammie. Her face had drained of all color, but
she'd drawn herself back up and forced herself to listen to
everything Roland had to confess.

A few moments ago, Roland had stopped speaking and
sat down, visibly slumping with dejection. He'd looked at her
with sorrow and apology; she had merely taken his face
between her hands and kissed his cheek.

Classy lady.

Case wasn't so charitable. He still itched to take out some
of his worry and frustration on Roland's face. Roland could
natter on until the end of the world about how he hadn't

intended to get Sammie into this mess. The fact remained that she'd never have been involved in any of it, except for him. Roland had a lot of sins to repent, but none more grievous than this.

The phone rang.

Bullhorn answered it. Case closed the distance between them, fighting the urge to yank it from Bullhorn's hand.

He looked up quickly at Case and nodded as he listened to the caller.

Case's heart raced. Maybe the waiting was over.

When Bullhorn hung up, all eyes were on him. "Gascoigne wants to meet with Roland—alone."

"The hell he will—" Case barked. "I'm going, too. I have to get to Sammie."

"He was very explicit, Case—no cops, no wires, and no one but Roland. He will consider exchanging Sammie for Roland—but only if his conditions are met."

Sammie's mother gasped and covered her mouth with the handkerchief crumpled in her hand. At another time, Case would have sympathized with her. She would undoubtedly lose one of the people she loved this night.

But it would not be Sammie. He would make sure of that.

Bullhorn sighed. "*Mon ami*, he was very clear on his conditions. However, I know you well. Tell me what help you need to carry out whatever plan is undoubtedly forming at this moment in that devious mind of yours."

Case flashed a grateful smile. And began outlining his ideas.

Etienne Gascoigne sighed as only a man who has many subordinates can. He wondered why he could not find the proper mix of logic and brutality in one man. He had made a simple request of Frenchy, to eliminate the threat from one young woman. Now, instead of one two-bit hustler to handle, Gascoigne had a spitting, angry *chatte* on his hands, to boot.

Frenchy had overstepped his bounds with this one. His innate brutality proved useful at times, but ham-fisted tactics were out of place here. This situation called for finesse. Frenchy's bestial desire to humiliate and violate the girl in retaliation for her defiance would lead them all to ruin if not controlled. He had succeeded in arousing rebellion in her already, according to Raymond. Killing her was not desirable, but negotiating with her might be impossible.

If that was so, killing her was the only option—she knew too much. Regrettable, perhaps, but necessary.

Gascoigne snapped out of his thoughts when he heard the warehouse door open.

Case silently thanked his old friend Hank Mallory as he scaled the last stretch to the warehouse roof. Hank was obsessed with rock climbing and had dragged Case along with him, swearing he'd love the challenge. Hank had been right, more than he could know. Though it had been several years and the gear Bullhorn had scared up wasn't top quality, the experience Case had gained in scaling heights and traversing difficult surfaces proved invaluable.

There was so much at stake. Fear for Sammie was a tight fist squeezing his throat. What if she wasn't here after all? What if Frenchy had—

No. He had to believe Gascoigne had ample reason to keep her alive. That he could control Frenchy.

But he could still picture her, pale and terrified when she remembered that bastard's brutal handling. If that sonofabitch laid another hand on her…

His grip on the rope slipped.

Swiftly he corrected. Steadied himself. Forced himself to ruthless control of his emotions.

Stay focused. It's the only way you can help her.

One foot upward, then the next.

When he reached the top of the warehouse, he scanned for Roland outside below. Assuring himself all was in place, Case made his way across the roof, looking for an opening.

Case neared the last two skylights, praying that one of them would give him a view into the space where Sammie was being held. He had to believe that Gascoigne would have her here to exchange as he had said. If that was a lie...

Case couldn't think about the implications of that. It would mean Sammie was being held somewhere else— another cranny in this city filled with dark corners—and God only knew how long it might take to find her. Or she was already—

No. He was going to find her. Save her. They'd had too little time together.

He wanted more. A lifetime more.

Then he heard the faint sound of a woman's voice, and his heart skipped. He approached slowly. He couldn't risk casting a shadow in the moonlight. Some of the other skylights he'd checked had been in varying stages of clouding, a couple nearly opaque. He hoped to heaven this one would be in better condition.

No more sounds from the space below, but a faint glow emitting through the skylight ahead raised his hopes. Careful to stay on the side opposite the moon, Case peered over the edge. Spotted a figure bent awkwardly on a cot in the room below.

The figure moved, and he saw it was Sammie.

She was alive.

He squeezed his eyes shut. Thank God. He'd found her.

He quickly scanned the room below for a way to enter.

Nothing promising. He'd have to return to the ground.

But he lingered for a second, simply absorbing the reality that she was here. He'd found her.

Then he realized she was working at the bindings on her ankles, and he had to smile.

What a woman. She'd never give up, not his Sammie.

Okay. Settle down now. He centered his thoughts on the task ahead and started to turn away to seek a way inside.

Movement at the edge of the room caught his eye.

Frenchy Pelletier lumbered into view.

Case's fists clenched. How he wanted a piece of that bastard.

He forced himself to remain still and observe—until Frenchy pinched one of Sammie's breasts with a vicious twist, and she cried out in pain. Red rage blinded Case, and he rose from his crouch—

Bits of gravel shifted, and the sound yanked him back from the bloodthirsty urge to beat Frenchy senseless.

He still hadn't seen where Gascoigne was. He had to have a complete picture of the setup before he went down there. It would do her no good for him to be taken hostage, too. Ruthlessly he steeled his mind to the task at hand, crushing all thoughts of revenge, knowing they would only distract him and not help Sammie at all.

Later, however…

He looked below once more, just in time to see Frenchy haul her to her feet with one brutal jerk. Sammie stumbled, then turned her head—

And spat right in Frenchy's face.

Damn it, Sammie, don't antagonize him.

She wouldn't go down without a fight, but Frenchy looked like he was spoiling for one. He hauled back and cuffed her hard on the side of the head.

Sammie swayed.

Frenchy yanked her upright, fist clenched to hit her

again—

A voice shouted at him, and he turned toward a door Case couldn't see. Frenchy bellowed a defiant response.

But he stopped hitting Sammie.

And dragged her out of the room.

Case's own fists clenched as he followed on the roof in the direction Frenchy had taken. The nearest skylight was cloudy and crackled. He could only make out several hazy figures below. Frustration seethed as he scanned the roof for the best place to enter the building near them. He couldn't afford to take the time to return to the far edge.

He hoped like hell Dolly had done her job with the sentry. He spared a quick glance and smiled thinly as he located Dolly on the ground below. Apparently, the sentry had proven relatively easy. No surprise there—few men could resist the woman who seduced entire audiences.

Dolly had taken to her role eagerly, thrilled to drive the Corvette Jerry Benson had provided. What a picture she must have made, hood up, draped over the engine, tiny skirt riding high on her thighs, drawing off the sentry by appealing to his instinct to help a very hot damsel in distress.

Sparky, Bullhorn's favorite bouncer, was assigned to make short work of the sentry once Dolly had the man's full attention. He would be tied up tight in Jerry's van nearby. Now it was up to Case to get inside.

"Well, *M'sieur* Bracewell, it seems we have a problem."

"I don't believe I've had the pleasure, *M'sieur*...Gascoigne?" Bracewell responded.

Gascoigne's eyes narrowed, then he looked down, flicking a speck of lint off the sleeve of the suit jacket he wore despite the sweltering heat of the night. In a voice suddenly devoid of all politeness, he said, "Let us not get cute, *mon ami*. Perhaps we can treat together, perhaps not, *c'est vrai? Mais*, do not play the fool with me, *comprends?*"

Bracewell said nothing, merely nodding.

"It seems to me that you have been perhaps a little too greedy, *n'est ce pas?* Had you continued to ply your petty little schemes, we would have been content to leave you alone. We always make a note of small-time operators like you, but usually your vision is too limited to cause us much trouble." He sighed loudly.

"But you, *M'sieur* Bracewell, chose to play in our arena, and we cannot have that. You are not one of us. You did not ask permission."

"Where is my niece?"

Gascoigne raised one eyebrow. "Ah, yes, the beauteous *Mademoiselle* St. Claire. She is resourceful, that one, eh?"

More sharply, Bracewell asked again. "Where is she, Gascoigne?"

"Do not presume to set the terms for our little conversation, *m'sieur.*" Gascoigne's voice grew cold. "You will know about her when I decide it is time, and not before. Now, *mon ami*, where are the files?"

"Not until I see Samantha," the other man insisted.

"Don't be a fool, Bracewell. I can simply take them from you."

"You could if I had them with me, but since I don't, you will need me to lead you to them."

Gascoigne narrowed his gaze. "A trick, *M'sieur* Bracewell? I had thought better of your intelligence. It would be a simple matter to beat the information out of you. Frankly, your niece has so frustrated Frenchy that I am certain he would be happy to do the honors."

Bracewell stared back as if daring him to do it.

"Ah, but Frenchy would far prefer to ply his trade upon the more delicate skin of your beautiful young niece, I think."

He clapped his hands. "Frenchy, *venez! Et la putain aussi.*"

Bracewell stiffened at the insult to his niece. Gascoigne heard him suck in his breath at the sight of her, blindfolded, bruised and battered. She stumbled on the uneven floor, and Frenchy didn't balk at the chance to be rough. He jerked her into the darkened room, cursing at her in a low growl. When they neared, Gascoigne nodded for him to stop just short of Bracewell.

Bracewell moved to embrace her.

Ray stepped in front of him.

"Oh, I believe you are close enough," said Gascoigne. "Do you have a good view? Such a pity, really. Frenchy does seem to harbor a very real resentment toward your niece, *M'sieur* Bracewell."

At the sound of her uncle's name, the girl's head came up quickly. She drew in a breath. Her mouth opened as if to speak, but Frenchy quickly squeezed her upper arm in warning. She fell silent, waiting.

Roland stiffened. "She's innocent in all this. Let her go, and I'll give you the files once she's free."

Gascoigne laughed, a short, bitter bark. "Oh, so easily you think to make demands? Why do you imagine I would believe you now? Besides, your pretty niece knows too much."

"She won't talk. She wants to protect her family."

"And when she tires of being silent? No, I think I would be most foolish to take that chance. I repeat, *m'sieur*. Why would I want to let her live?"

"Because I have given copies of the files to someone who will make sure they wind up in the hands of the U.S. District Attorney and the bank examiners if she is harmed."

For the first time, Sammie allowed herself a little hope. Uncle

Roland was a schemer, and right now, she was happy to have him on her side. He seemed to have neatly boxed Gascoigne into a corner. With effort, she schooled her features to remain neutral.

Gascoigne spoke up. "Very nice, Bracewell. A neat move on your part." His voice hardened. "Frenchy, she's all yours."

Sammie gasped.

Frenchy jerked her up close and ripped off the blindfold, his hot, fetid breath turning her stomach.

Fear spiked. She didn't understand what had just happened.

Uncle Roland shouted, "Gascoigne, it won't work. I can't reverse my instructions for the files. Tell him to leave her alone!"

"How do I know that, *mon ami?* No, I think a little time for Frenchy to work might prove most instructive. Go ahead, Frenchy. Do what you will."

Frenchy ripped her camisole down the front—

A splintering crack. A roar from above.

Case dropped to the floor and rolled, regaining his balance quickly. The gun in his hand pointed right at Frenchy's heart.

Frenchy froze for a second. "You!" He yanked Sammie in front of him.

A deadly knife appeared in his hand. He held it to her throat. "Go ahead, you bastard, give me an excuse. Drop the gun, or she suffers for it."

"Samantha!" Uncle Roland charged toward her. "Leave her alone!"

Ray whipped out a pistol.

Uncle Roland threw himself the last few feet—

Ray fired.

Her uncle crumpled at Gascoigne's feet.

Sammie screamed.

Frenchy crushed the breath out of her.

His knife was a hot sting as he pressed it into her throat.

Case watched the struggle on her face. If he dropped his weapon, she was dead. So was he.

But he needed time for reinforcements to arrive. "Hang on, sweetheart." He didn't look at her, instead casting around in his mind for a way to break the deadlock.

From the corner of his eye, he could see Ray edging toward him. He thought Gascoigne still stood in the same place. Case didn't dare take his eyes off Frenchy to check.

"I mean it, *cochon*, drop the gun." Frenchy pressed the blade into Sammie's skin again, drawing more blood.

Damn it. Case dropped the gun.

"Case, no—" Sammie moaned in anguish.

"Now kick it over this way," Frenchy ordered.

Case kicked it, never taking his eyes off Frenchy, watching for his opening.

Suddenly, the door flew open. Dolly's voice rang out, "Roland, sugar, why did you leave me waiting out there?"

Frenchy's head whipped around toward the sound of Dolly's voice.

Sammie shoved backward and fouled his balance.

Case leaped and grabbed the hand holding the knife. Frenchy couldn't fight him and hold onto Sammie, too. "Get down, Sammie!"

She dropped to the floor and rolled out of the way.

Case's muscles strained as he squeezed Frenchy's wrist, trying to make him drop the knife. He couldn't see Ray anymore, and Ray still had shots left. He struggled to turn the stocky Frenchy to keep him between Ray and himself.

Bullhorn's man Sparky charged through the door.

He aimed and fired behind Case.

Ray spun around from the hit to the shoulder and fell to the floor nearby.

Sparky trained his gun on Gascoigne, daring him to move.

The sound of the shot made Frenchy flinch just enough to loosen his hold on the knife. Case threw his weight into Frenchy and knocked him to the floor. The knife skittered across the concrete.

Case rose and plowed his fist right into Frenchy's face. Pounded him again with all the fury he'd built up over the long, anxious hours of searching for Sammie.

Sammie cried out, "Somebody, please—finish untying me!"

Case heard footsteps and whipped his head toward her just as Dolly reached her.

Frenchy took advantage of the distraction. Leg-whipped Case onto his back and rose over him. Landed several sharp blows to Case's head and ribs.

Dolly screamed. "Sammie, no!"

Case rallied. Adrenaline surged, and he reared up, throwing Frenchy over on his back. As he raised his fist to land another blow, a shot rang out from behind him, plowing into the concrete near Frenchy's head.

"What the—" Case turned, one hand still squeezing Frenchy's throat.

Sammie approached, Case's gun aimed straight at Frenchy's head. Her hands trembled and her voice shook. "Move away, Case."

It was the voice of a woman he'd never met. A woman who'd been pushed too far.

"Sammie…" He made sure Sparky had everyone in his sights, then released Frenchy and rose, approaching her slowly. "Let me have the gun, sweetheart," he said gently.

"I can't do that. He'll never stop. He'll come after me again." The agony in her voice raked furrows into his soul. She was everything to him, and he'd failed to keep her safe.

He closed in, speaking in a low, soothing tone. "Honey, I am more sorry than you can know that I wasn't here to protect you, but I will die before I'll let him hurt you again." When she wouldn't look at him but took another step toward Frenchy, he tried again. "Give me the gun, Sammie. You are too good for this. You don't deserve to have killing on your conscience."

Everyone in the room went still as statues, watching the drama play out before them. Sammie clutched at her torn blouse with one hand as she struggled to hold the heavy gun level with the other, tears rolling down her cheeks.

She raised her eyes to meet Case's gaze. The torment in them tore at his heart.

He could see the ice princess trying to emerge once more, but her edges were badly frayed.

"I—" Her voice caught on a sob. "He hurt me so much, Case. I tried, but I couldn't stop him. I was too weak."

"You're not weak. You're the bravest damn person I know, sweetheart. Please don't do this to yourself. You won't want to live with the knowledge that you've killed someone, even scum like him." He held out a hand for the gun. "Please. He doesn't deserve the break, but you do."

Sammie shuddered. Took a deep, ragged breath.

The moment dragged out.

Finally she lowered the gun.

Case took it from her and wrapped her in his arms. She fell against him with a broken sob, and Case held her tightly.

Frenchy uncoiled himself from the floor and launched himself at Case.

Case whirled and brought up the pistol, shoving Sammie behind him as he fired.

Sparky fired, as well.

Frenchy dropped to the ground.

Sammie sank to the floor beside the still Frenchy, wrapping her arms around herself, rocking. Shaking visibly. "I hate you. Don't touch me…don't you ever touch me," she sobbed.

Case bent to her. Drew her into his arms and stroked her back. As he comforted, her sobs slowly died away. She huddled against him, trembling violently.

He looked over at Dolly, who knelt beside Roland, checking for vital signs. She shook her head.

Case grimaced. Roland had much to answer for, but he didn't deserve to pay with his life.

Case looked over Sammie's head at Gascoigne, silently asking a question.

Gascoigne held his hands up, shrugging eloquently as he eyed the gun Sparky had trained on him. "It appears we are at an impasse, *m'sieur*. My quarrel was with Bracewell, not with you. Since he is dead, the situation has altered."

Sammie's head reared as Gascoigne's words penetrated. She turned to look at Roland, horror-stricken at the sight of the growing pool of blood. "No!" She pulled away from Case and ran to her uncle, kneeling beside him, feeling for a pulse.

Dolly gently laid a hand on her arm. "He's gone, honey."

Sammie dropped her head as the tears began to flow.

Case went to her.

"He always loved me, I know he did. He did a lot of bad things, Case, but he always loved me."

Everything she'd suffered was Roland's fault, but if she needed to remember Roland's love and forget his mistakes, Case would not be the one to make her face them.

After a long moment, Sammie straightened and looked squarely at Gascoigne. "So where do we go from here?"

It would be naïve to think Gascoigne could ever be made to pay for all that had happened, Case knew. He'd never been visibly involved, probably orchestrating all of this from a safe distance. People like Gascoigne operated with impunity, their tentacles extending even into the law enforcement establishment.

But Sammie surprised him with a challenge to Gascoigne.

"I believe Uncle Roland's claim that he had files hidden, to be released if anything happens to me."

Gascoigne sighed, acknowledging her point with a nod. "And, my dear, even if I am taken out of the picture, my friends can keep an eye on your family. We have long memories. Will you dare risk them by talking to the authorities?"

Sammie studied him in silence.

Finally she shook her head no.

But Case bet she wouldn't give up searching for an answer. Nor would he.

"Then, as I told your valiant young man here, it appears that we are at an impasse. If you do not interfere with our Mr. Whitehead, we will not bother your family. You may continue your life as it was. A fair bargain, I think—live and let live. All we ever wanted was to be left alone to conduct our business in peace."

It was the best offer they could hope for, however much it stuck in his craw.

Apparently Sammie recognized that, too. "With one condition first. You will have Whitehead erase Case's debt to the bank."

Gascoigne waved a negligent hand. "Small change. Then, do we have an agreement?"

Her jaw hardened. "All right, *M'sieur* Gascoigne. Live and let live."

At least for now, Case thought.

Then Ray moaned and struggled to sit up as he returned to consciousness. Sparky kept his pistol trained between Ray and Gascoigne, waiting for a signal from Case.

Case looked over at him. "Sparky, please escort Gascoigne and this scumbag out to their car and let them know where to find their sentry." He jerked Ray to his feet. Ray groaned.

He grabbed Ray by the shirtfront, yanking him up close, growling his demand. "Gascoigne, I don't ever want this scum or any like him anywhere near Sammie—are we clear on that? Your bargain is with Sammie, not with me. I don't give a damn about my note or what happens to her family, only that she is safe." His words were directed at Gascoigne, but his menacing glare was aimed straight at Ray.

"You are very arrogant, *M'sieur* Marshall. However, I have many other things to occupy my attention and that of my men. We will hear quickly enough if she has broken our agreement. Unless that happens, my men will remain otherwise occupied."

It would have to be enough, for the moment. As insurance, Case probed Ray's gaze to make sure the man understood his intentions, waiting for an acknowledgment.

Ray nodded, then jerked away, following Gascoigne out the door.

Chapter Twenty-One

C ase looked across Roland's gravesite to discover Armand St. Claire studying him. He gazed back steadily, knowing his measure was being taken. He'd met Sammie's father a few days before when he'd taken her home to her family, but the circumstances had hardly been ideal, given what they'd been asking her father to do.

Case suspected the man didn't like the stalemate with Gascoigne any better than he did, but St. Claire's desire to avoid publicity worked in their favor. He'd agreed to go along with the story Case and Sammie had devised, that her uncle had been killed by Sammie's kidnapper, who escaped without capture.

The search for that kidnapper would be fruitless, Case was certain. Sammie had insisted to the police that she'd been blindfolded the whole time and could provide no helpful clues. Apparently Gascoigne had cleaned up the scene so thoroughly that they would have no evidence to go on.

Case also suspected that Gascoigne had used his illegal ties to law enforcement to apply pressure from his end. When combined with Armand St. Claire's political pull, the case wasn't likely to receive serious follow-through. It suited everyone's purposes to have Roland regarded as a hero, taking some of the tarnish off the reputation of a man who'd been a thorn in St. Claire's side for years.

All of which was fine with Case—until a wall had been thrown up between him and Sammie.

He hadn't seen her since that night he'd restored her to her family, however he'd tried. He wasn't sure why he was even still in New Orleans, but when he'd called to let Wiley and Linnie Mae know what had happened, Wiley had encouraged him to remain a while longer. "A few days won't make a difference, one way or the other, Case. Sammie needs you more."

Case had his doubts. She stood across a crowd of mourners, closed-off and remote, a beautiful china doll who bore no resemblance to the woman in pink Keds. Something had broken inside her, but he couldn't get close enough to her to find out if he could fix whatever it was.

She'd been swallowed up into a world to which he had no entry.

He'd tried to get through to her mother, but though Mrs. St. Claire had seemed sympathetic, she'd refused to call Sammie downstairs, insisting that her daughter was exhausted and needed to rest.

Against every instinct he had, Case had backed off, but he couldn't give up without one more try.

Today was it. He'd confront her. Refuse to let her guard dogs intervene until he'd spoken directly to her.

Maybe she'd had a reality check, seen him for who he was. Understood, as he did, that she was out of his league. That his future wasn't bright enough for her.

If so, he'd head on back to the ranch and accept that it was over between them.

Back to the ranch and the lonely life stretching endlessly ahead.

But not without one more try. As the service ended, he started through the crowd toward her.

Someone stepped into his path.

Armand St. Claire regarded him silently. Case stared right

back. At last Sammie's father spoke. "Mr. Marshall, I am not without resources to protect my family, even in these circumstances."

Case frowned, waiting for him to make his point.

For the first time, the icy, superior St. Claire looked uneasy. Uncertain. "What I cannot do is repair my daughter's broken heart. I have watched her closely over these last few days, and I have seen her grow steadily more and more listless." His gaze intensified. "My daughter cares for you, Mr. Marshall. Whether or not that is wise is not my choice to make. If I could heal her myself, I would."

Case blinked. This was not at all what he'd expected.

But he wouldn't waste the opportunity to make his case. "I love her, Mr. St. Claire."

"Ah, but is your love strong enough to convince her that she does not have to give you up, in order to save you?"

"What?" Case couldn't believe his ears.

"You have a difficult task ahead of you, Marshall. My daughter believes that her very presence imparts danger to those she loves. My question to you is, are you afraid of the curse she believes she carries?" He paused, then added, "If I am not sadly mistaken, she is planning to disappear from us all."

Case's heart seized in his chest. "The hell she is." Every protective instinct he had roared to life. "I would give my life to keep her safe. I'm not afraid of what's hanging over her." Then he shook his head. "But I can't give Sammie the luxuries she has here. Not now, and maybe not ever." His chin lifted in challenge.

Armand St. Claire exhaled in a gust. "In the last few days, I've had to do some hard thinking. Samantha has talked for a long time of how meaningless my lifestyle is. I'm finally listening. Seeing my daughter's bruised body, knowing her inner pain and the torment she's suffered, I've had to come to terms with just how little my wealth and social position mean at the worst time of her life." His gaze held apology. "My daughter, it seems, is wiser than her father. Money is not so important to her, and anyway, she has plenty of her own."

"I don't want her money."

"That is for you and Samantha to work out. The point is that my daughter has apparently found what she's been missing on your ranch—with you."

Case blinked. Hope stirred.

"It pains me to admit that you would once have been my last choice in a mate for my daughter, but there it is." Armand St. Claire held out his hand. "I'll never be able to properly express my deep gratitude to you for saving my daughter's life. What I can do for you, and for her, is to give you my blessing and my support." His eyes pleaded. "I beg you, Mr. Marshall—take her home with you and keep her safe. You have my promise that Gascoigne will pay somewhere down the road, if it takes until my dying breath. I, too, have friends who will watch and wait."

Case accepted the handshake as he tried to absorb how his earlier despair had just been turned on its head. "I will guard her with my life. I also promise you that I will do everything possible to make her life comfortable, but above all, she will never lack for love."

"Persuading her to go with you won't be easy. She is convinced that her presence puts those she loves in danger. She has her own valor, and she will do what she thinks is right."

"I've had ample demonstration of her courage, but I don't give up easily." Especially not now, not when he had reason to fight.

"I wish you well as you try to convince her not to sacrifice what she wants most to protect those she loves." Her father's eyes misted. "Samantha understood long before her father that love is all that's truly important."

Then his gaze shifted to the side.

Sammie drew near.

203

Case drank in the sight of her as her father left them. His breath caught in his throat as the blue eyes he loved so much stared back into his.

Time stood still as he hungrily scanned the face so dear to him. She looked worn out, her eyelids puffy and reddened from crying. Her face was hollow, purple smudges shadowing the delicate skin beneath her eyes, but to him, she'd never been more beautiful than she was at that moment. He ached to hold her and give her comfort.

Desire still simmered under the surface—it always would. But he could wait for passion. He wanted to share so much more with this woman—laughter and sorrow, children and old age, good times and bad—the full range of human existence. Whatever the future held would be welcome with her at his side.

He had come too close to losing her forever. However long it took, he would wait her out.

"Sammie." He moved to her.

She took a step back, out of reach.

Though she drew away from Case, Sammie's heart ached with the force of her longing. His was the face she loved most of all. With every fiber of her being, she yearned to fall into his arms and escape from everything but the man before her.

But she was tainted, potential poison to everyone around her. She and Gascoigne were at a stand-off, yes, and it might hold for years, but she'd never forget the seamy world she'd been forced to enter. She would never expose those she loved to that horror. She'd given it all a lot of thought since that terrible night in the warehouse, and she'd decided to go away to someplace where no one knew her and no one she loved could be hurt.

It was the safest course for everyone. Maybe Gascoigne would forget her if she stayed away. Certainly she would draw the danger away from her family, and Case and the ranch would also be safe.

The very thought of never again seeing all those she'd come to love back in Texas sent a bittersweet pang through her heart.

But that was nothing to the dread that filled her at the thought of never seeing this man again.

"Sammie," repeated that voice that went straight to her heart. "How are you?"

"I'm fine."

"You're not fine. How could you be? I will never forgive myself that Frenchy ever put a hand on you—"

She had to touch him then. "Case, no. None of this is on you. Without you…" She had to close her eyes as memory swamped her. She opened them again. "You saved me. I owe you everything."

His jaw flexed. "You owe me nothing. You forget that I threw you out, that I cast you into that nightmare without giving you a chance to explain—" He looked away, his features hard and angry in self-reproach.

"I'm all right now. I'm unharmed, all because of you."

"Are you?" he challenged. His laugh was bitter. "How can you possibly be all right after what you went through?" He shook his head. "I'm insane to have even considered—" He broke off.

"Considered what?"

Those gorgeous green eyes rose to pin hers. "Asking you to come home with me. Make a life with me. Letting me love you to my last breath."

Her eyes filled with tears. "I wish I could," she whispered.

"Why can't you?"

"Because I'm…poison. I've already brought so much trouble your way. I can't risk bringing more. I really—I have to go." She started to turn away before she broke completely.

"Sammie, look at me." He grasped her shoulders and turned her toward him. "That's not your decision to make."

"I know what's right. Gascoigne could still—"

"I know exactly what Gascoigne is capable of, and I'm not afraid. Do you think Wiley would be? Or Linnie Mae? You seriously think they wouldn't fight the devil himself for you?"

"But, Case—"

"No 'buts' about it. You have leverage over Gascoigne. You're at a stalemate, one that will probably last until he or Whitehead is dead. We'll keep working at it—maybe there's some way to bring him to justice. And look at it this way: if you're out of New Orleans, he'll have even less reason to think about you. Face it, sweetheart, how much further from New Orleans can you get than my sorry excuse for a ranch?"

"Don't you talk like that. I love your ranch. Love every one of those people."

"And me?" he asked, his heart in his eyes. "Never mind." Then he looked away. "I'm not a good bargain, Sammie. I can't promise I could ever offer you anything to resemble the luxury you've had all your life, not that I won't try like hell, but ranching is always a crapshoot. It's not an easy life, and you'd be crazy to want it. Hell, I don't know why I want it."

"But you do," she said. "And so do I."

His head whipped up. "Why?"

"Because I love you?" She smiled at last. "Here's my reality, Case. I've had those luxuries, and they don't convey happiness. I've been a fish out of water for years and never understood why, but now I do. I've never felt so at home as I felt at the ranch. I miss everyone so—" She halted. "Are you really sure about this? I couldn't bear it if anything—"

"Nothing is certain in this life, but I don't take chances lightly with those I love. I want you to come with me more than I've ever wanted anything. I will promise that I'll give you everything I am and all that I can provide, to my last breath on earth." He drew both her hands between his as though making a vow. "Please...say yes. Say you'll come home with me. That you'll let me do my best to love you as you deserve."

Sammie's eyes swam and her throat filled, but she managed to speak. "I want that so much."

"Then take it. Take me."

She hesitated, but there was a world in those green eyes, a world she desperately wanted to inhabit. "You're sure."

"I'm sure. Come home, Sammie. Say yes."

One unsteady breath, then a deeper one. "Yes. Oh, yes, Case. I love you so much. I'll make you so happy, I promise."

She threw her arms around him, and he lifted her off her feet, twirling her in a joyous circle. "You already have, sweetheart."

Then they both realized that they were still in a cemetery in plain sight.

She grinned at him. He grinned back.

And carried her behind a huge old oak.

He paused his gaze solemn. "You will never be alone again, I swear it. And you will have more love than you know what to do with."

Then he lowered his mouth to hers.

And after a long, dark night, her world shone bright as the sun.

Epilogue

"That much male beauty in one spot should probably be illegal," murmured Lorie Marshall.

"No kidding," said her sister-in-law Elena. "I'll take the hot one on the right."

Sammie glanced up from caressing her one-week-old son's head and sighed. "I get dibs on the middle one." Case stood there, flanked by his two equally tall cousins, surveying the vista before them. Josh was a handsome and hot film star and Quinn one of the most compelling men she'd ever met, but Case was the one she'd choose even if the others were available and not crazy in love with their wives.

Though he'd been in touch with his cousins ever since Quinn had given him advice about finding her when she'd been abducted, it had been a big step for Case to invite them here. He'd want to meet his cousins on equal footing, and securing the ranch had taken some time.

They'd done it, however. Even though he still refused to use any of her money, between her knowledge of the financial world and Case's innovations, the trucking company was up on its feet again. Just a month before, Case had made his last run, happy to turn the driving over to others who didn't want to be home as much as he did, he told her.

"I'll settle for the dreamboat with the long hair," Lorie said, then laughed, naughty and low. "There cannot be three luckier ladies on the planet, you think?"

"And they make such beautiful babies," Sammie said, drawn once more to the sleeping infant in her arms. Randall Armand Marshall bore Wiley's middle name for his first, and one would think Wiley had given birth to the boy, he'd been so proud.

"They sure do." Lorie turned back to admire young Randy. "Enough to keep you from selling them to the circus when they turn into hellions like ours." Her affectionate smile gave the lie to her words as she glanced toward the corral where her rambunctious five-year-old twins, Antonio and Emilio, competed with David for her thirteen-year-old son Grant's attention as Grant talked horses with Wiley.

"Sammie, Sammie!" Jennifer and her new best friend, Lorie and Quinn's daughter Clarissa, raced over. "Randy needs to see the new kittens! Can the other babies come, too?"

Josh and Elena's own infant daughter Consuela and toddler son Eli were being rocked by Linnie Mae and Josh's Tía Consuela on the porch right behind them.

"Elena?" Sammie deferred the decision.

"Perhaps later for them, *niña*," Elena answered the girl.

"They're just babies," Clarissa explained. "And Eli gets cranky if he misses his nap, right, Aunt Elena?"

"You're right. But maybe you could show me instead?"

"Great!" Each girl took a hand and led Elena to the barn.

"Speaking of naps," said Case, coming up from beside Sammie. "You had a long night last night. How come you're not taking a nap, too?" His voice wasn't convincingly stern, and the twinkle in his eyes was anything but.

"We have company," she protested. "And you didn't get any more sleep than I did. You're the one who got up to fetch him and change him every time."

He waggled his eyebrows. "So you need a napping partner?"

She smiled into his mischievous eyes. "We wouldn't be

very good hosts."

"Get a room, you two," called out Josh.

"Hey, he's my older cousin. Gotta listen to good advice," Case said.

"Go on with you." She knew her cheeks were flaming.

Case plucked their son from her arms, pausing to dip his head and steal a kiss from her. He winked at her as he turned away, his expression tender as he cuddled his son, walking back to rejoin Josh and Quinn.

Sammie couldn't help a sigh, watching him.

Lorie chuckled. "The sight of a gorgeous alpha male holding a baby in his arms is guaranteed to turn a woman's heart to mush."

"It is. I am so lucky." She'd come so close to losing all this. To sacrificing it out of fear. Thank heavens Case wouldn't listen.

"Case thinks he's the lucky one. From what Quinn has told me about Case's father, his life was no cakewalk."

"I'm going to make sure it is from now on."

Lorie sat down beside her. "So, no second thoughts about leaving the high life?"

"Not a single one." Sammie turned to her. "You?" Lorie had been a star in her own right, appearing on television with Josh early in his career. Now she was a midwife with a thriving practice.

"I'd have to be crazy to give up what I have…and my mama didn't raise a fool. There's something about those Marshall men, isn't there?"

"There certainly is," Sammie agreed. "And it's not just the outrageous good looks."

"It's not." The woman who once took daytime television by storm and had won an Emmy nodded. "But those good looks sure don't suck."

Sammie burst out laughing, and Lorie joined her.

Three outrageously good-looking males turned to see

what was so funny.

Sammie and her fellow Marshall woman only smiled mysteriously and blew them kisses.

When she'd been running for her life, could she have ever imagined such happiness?

No. But was she going to cherish every second of the bounty she had?

Absolutely.

"Thank you for making the trip over here," she said to Lorie. "Case needs family."

"He's got us, whether he wants us or not," Lorie responded. "Let's go grab us each a good-looking Marshall man." She winked. "Elena's on her own."

Grinning, Lorie rose, and Sammie followed her. Maybe she'd never imagined so much happiness coming out of such danger.

But her mama hadn't raised a fool either.

With a smile, Sammie walked toward the love she'd been waiting for all her life.

Her very own dark angel smiled back at her, cradling their future in his strong arms.

~THE END~

Thank you for letting me share my stories with you!

The earlier stories in this series are TEXAS REFUGE and TEXAS STAR, about Case's cousins Quinn and Josh. If you liked The Marshalls series, the Marshalls couples also show up in the Sweetgrass Springs series, especially TEXAS DREAMS, TEXAS CHRISTMAS BRIDE and TEXAS STRONG.

TEXAS REFUGE

Rancher Quinn Marshall is haunted after nearly dying in a failed attempt to save his sister. The last thing the former homicide detective wants is another woman to watch over, but someone important to his brother is in trouble, and Quinn's basic nature is to protect. Soap opera star Lorie Chandler has already lost her husband to an obsessed fan and now her son is the madman's new target.

While the police hunt the killer, Quinn's rugged Texas ranch is the ideal hiding place for Lorie and her child. Neither Quinn nor Lorie expects the explosive heat or the powerful emotion that flares to life in his canyon refuge, yet there is no future for them and both are painfully aware that their time together can only be temporary. When the madman finds them, Quinn's sole focus is on keeping Lorie and the boy he's come to love safe, even though his success will mean that he will have to give them up to a life where he cannot belong.

TEXAS STAR

Sexiest Man Alive Josh Marshall is on his way home to Texas when he rescues a woman on the run. In contrast to the many women crushing on him all over the world, this woman does not trust him and wants nothing to do with him, seeking to escape every time his back is turned.

Elena Navarro is running from an abusive husband with criminal ties. Terrified to trust anyone, she finds Josh's tender care a miracle, but his fame and celebrity status could be a death sentence for them both. When echoes of a shared past life threaten, Josh questions his sanity, but he's a white knight to the core and cannot stop trying to help her, even at the risk of his life.

If you enjoyed TEXAS DANGER, I would be very grateful if you would help others find this book by recommending it in such places as GOODREADS, BOOKBUB and the retailer's site where you bought it. If you would like to be informed when my next release is available or get news of special prices on my books, please sign up for my newsletter at www.jeanbrashear.com and you can also follow me on Bookbub.

I love hearing from you, so please contact me through any of the options at the end of this book.

Thanks!
Jean

Please enjoy this excerpt from the first Sweetgrass Springs story, TEXAS ROOTS:

What had possessed her mother to keep Sweetgrass Springs a secret for thirty-two years? To tell her that they had no family?

Scarlett Ross pressed the accelerator and tried to think about that mystery instead of the fear that tangled beneath her breastbone: would she be safe there?

She crested the last hill, the tiny town a small diamond of light cushioned in flocked green velvet as the smudged violet of night stole over the Texas Hill Country. January here was far kinder than in New York. While the grass was a flaxen hue and some trees were only bare trunks and branches, many were still green.

The road curved left, right, left again, while Sweetgrass Springs winked in and out of view. Dead tired from the long drive fleeing the wreckage of her life in Manhattan, Scarlett longed for a meal and a bed. Best she'd been able to tell from the limited information available online, however, only the meal would be available in this town of fifteen hundred sixty-seven. The nearest motel was an hour back the way she'd come, but after running full-speed halfway across the country, Scarlett couldn't bear to wait another night to find out if she, in fact, was not alone in this world, after all.

She had nowhere else to go. Her career was in ruins and the media hounded her every step, screaming for juicy details of her affair with a drug lord. For two years she'd been a meteor on the rise in the only city that mattered...and now she was a star in a tragedy. A farce, except that a cop had died in the raid.

She wasn't a criminal...but she was criminally stupid, no question. How could she not have seen? How could she have blithely accepted Andre's assurances that it was his love for her that made him want to showcase her talents in the gem of a restaurant into which she'd put her heart and soul?

Instead, Mirelle had been simply a front for illegal activities that had gone on under her nose. And she'd never once, in the whole two years, suspected. Never wanted to look. She'd simply been grateful for the focus, the distraction from her grief. His offer had come right after she'd lost her only family, and she'd boxed up her mother's effects without a look. Instead of immediately leaving for parts unknown as her mother had always done when things got crazy, she'd tried something radical: she'd planned to stay in one place. She'd been too devastated to think straight, had been ripe pickings for Andre's machinations.

She'd been grateful, so grateful for the rescue. She'd lost her only compass in a life spent on the move, and she'd welcomed the chaos and endless work that allowed her not to think. The solace of someone who cared.

Except Andre hadn't really cared, had he? She'd been a dupe, and she'd walked into his trap with gratitude, playing her part to perfection.

The velvet-lined trap had sprung just when her future seemed brightest, when she was at last emerging from grief and loneliness.

Only to wind up in handcuffs, with her picture on the front page of the newspaper and featured on the evening newscast. Andre had escaped scot-free, no doubt on some tropical island drinking mai tais with a new idiot, while she stood holding the bag because he'd put her name on the more damaging documents.

And she'd thought him so sweet to both bankroll the venture and give her Mirelle.

She'd been trapped in New York for twelve days while the District Attorney had bled her brain dry, then she'd been freed under the stipulation that she'd testify against Andre and his cohorts—should they ever be found. On one of many sleepless nights, wandering the apartment filled with hated memories of Andre, in desperation she'd dragged out a box of her mother's things. There, in her mother's girlhood diary, a stunned Scarlett had discovered family. In Texas, of all places, one of the few states she and her mother had not lived.

A grandmother, still alive, from what little Scarlett could determine…a treasure she'd longed for all her life. Why Georgia Ross had never spoken one word of Sweetgrass Springs or family was reason for caution, certainly, but Scarlett had decided that once she had her life back together, she would seek the answers she craved to the riddle of her mother's past.

Then came a late night visit from two very scary men there to silence her before she could testify. Thanks to her drunken neighbors' screaming battle, the cops had shown up next door, and she'd been left with the memory of a knife to her throat and a whispered warning.

Scarlett's timeline had abruptly sped up. She'd left town within hours.

Texas had been the only place she could think of to go.

To pay a visit to the grandmother she'd never known existed and to buy herself a few days to think what to do next.

She had nowhere else to go. No options.

Okay, she still had her skills, and there might be some corner of the world where no one read the headlines. Truth to tell, New York only thought of itself as the center of the universe—there were other foodie towns like Santa Fe or San Francisco, other places where her skills could take her. Where the confidence she'd once had in spades could land her a new position.

If only she weren't so tired. So scared.

What if her grandmother wanted nothing to do with her? Why had her mother kept her family a secret? A million things could be wrong, so many ways this could go bad.

She was alone as never before in her life. Until two years ago, there had always been her mother. They had moved often, yes, but they were a team, they were solid. As long as they'd had each other, they needed little more.

How Scarlett missed her.

In Georgia's place remained only a mystery.

Who was her mother? Why did she leave here and never say one word to Scarlett about this place, when they had always been so close? Why did Scarlett have to find out about it when she could ask no questions? Was there some reason she should stay away, too? Her mother had been footloose but not foolish.

It was only a meal. A chance to reconnoiter. She didn't have to say anything to a soul.

The road ran alongside a ribbon of water, and a little further she could see it wind through the town next to a three-story courthouse that formed one corner of the town square, most of the buildings dark and closed, only a handful of them taller than one story. It was surely the tiniest town she'd ever seen.

She rounded the corner, and one building spilled out light

in welcome. Ruby's Café. Owned by one Ruby Gallagher.

The grandmother Scarlett had never known existed.

Scarlett sucked in a deep breath for courage. She'd been the new kid countless times.

But her mother had always had her back.

Nonsense. I'll be okay. I'm a grown woman. It won't matter if she can't love me.

…Excerpt from TEXAS ROOTS *by Jean Brashear* © *2013.*

The TEXAS HEROES series:

THE GALLAGHERS OF MORNING STAR

Dalton Wheeler vanished from Morning Star, Texas nearly forty years ago under suspicion of murder, leaving behind him a trail of secrets, scandal and lives torn apart in the wake of his reported death. The woman he loved married another, and life went on.

Now the main characters in this tragedy are all gone, and in the wake of the final man's last will and testament, the past has roared back with a vengeance. Secrets will be revealed and the lives of four people will be shattered as they learn that who they are and where they come from is not at all what they always believed.

Texas Secrets: Former SEAL Boone Gallagher returns to the only home he's ever known only to find that the ranch has been willed to a stranger who doesn't want it—and he must keep her there for thirty days, or it will be lost to them both.

Texas Lonely: A loner who's lost faith in love is the only hope for a mother and child on the run

Texas Bad Boy: Disgraced bad boy has his chance for revenge against the beautiful society girl who chose money over his love

THE MARSHALLS

Emotional and suspenseful stories of the sexy, gorgeous Marshall brothers—one deeply private, one world-famous—and their equally captivating bad boy cousin, each in his own way, a woman's dream lover…

Texas Refuge: Haunted former detective is the only sanctuary for an actress being stalked by a madman

Texas Star: Sexiest Man Alive becomes a white knight for a woman who keeps trying to escape him

Texas Danger: Down on his luck rancher is the only hope for a socialite on the run from the mob

THE GALLAGHERS OF SWEETGRASS SPRINGS

Nestled in the Texas Hill Country, tiny Sweetgrass Springs was founded by four veterans of the Texas Revolution, and for over a century the town and their ranches grew and prospered. Nowadays, however, too many of the town's children leave for the big city as soon as they can escape, and Sweetgrass is barely hanging on. The heart and soul of Sweetgrass is Ruby Gallagher, once a scandal for bearing a child out of wedlock and refusing to identify the father. Her daughter vanished from Sweetgrass right after high school, but Ruby, owner of community gathering place Ruby's Café, remains, keeping vigil, hoping for her daughter's return. She is fighting to save her ancestors' legacy, but the town is dying, and it's breaking Ruby's heart.

Texas Roots: A Paris-trained chef on the run finds Texas family she never knew existed and a sexy cowboy she doesn't dare love

Texas Wild: Sexy SEAL turned Hollywood stuntman returns home to find his buddy's little sister all grown up

Texas Dreams: Take two reluctant brides and two frustrated grooms, mix with both clans of Gallaghers and season with a SEAL or three, a movie star, a Hollywood Barbie and a country music giant—and get not one but two surprise weddings

Texas Rebel: A former rebellious teen turned billionaire's reunion with his teenage sweetheart and a secret baby he never knew about

Texas Blaze: What happens when a shark lawyer in stilettos has a fling with a hot firefighter determined to find Suzy Homemaker?

Texas Christmas Bride: All he wants is the girl he thought he'd lost forever.

THE BOOK BABES BOXED SET

The Book Babes reading group began as five women wanting to talk books—but now they've become family. There's romance author Ava Sinclair, organizer and backbone; happily-married mother of five Ellie Preston, the heart of the group; elegant art gallery owner Sylvie Everett; single mom and sociology professor Luisa Martinez; and ambitious attorney Laken Foster, the wild child of the bunch. For several years now, they've met monthly and discussed the current book a little—and dissected their lives and loves far more often.

But now change is rippling through the group, begun by Laken's restlessness with her freewheeling life of serial hookups and sent into hyperdrive by Ava's suddenly-hot career, while Luisa's abusive ex tries to reclaim their teenage son and Sylvie faces her mother's decline. But it's when Ellie takes her first step into life after her children fly the nest and falls under the spell of the sexy artist who's teaching her to paint that the group's orbit begins to wobble on its axis, and life—for all of them and the men they love—will never be the same.

And then there's the surprise Sweetgrass Springs connection…

MORE SWEETGRASS SPRINGS STORIES:

Texas Hope: Can two brothers who never knew each other existed overcome the secrets of a woman who abandoned one son and lied to the other?

Texas Strong: Can a man who's never trusted anyone and a woman who's trusted all the wrong men defy the odds and open their hearts to each other?

Texas Sweet: When a stranger who holds the keys to her identity arrives in town, will the girl everyone knows as Brenda come to terms with her past or run again?

Be Mine This Christmas: The man he's become is not the boy she once knew—and he may never forgive her, once he knows the secret she's been concealing.

Texas Charm: He's a country superstar; she's a small town waitress. When the real world slams into their reverie, whose heart will be the one to break? (Contains an original song written for this book)

Texas Magic: One billionaire...one tomboy...one night of magic. Miracle or mirage?

Be My Midnight Kiss: It's New Year's Eve...and now or never for these two hearts

LONE STAR LOVERS

Heart-tugging, action-packed and passionate stories of the close-knit Sullivan/Sandoval family of four brothers and one sister and a related family separated for many years after three sisters were orphaned.

Texas Heartthrob: Hollywood's hottest star is a man in disguise when he encounters a woman who's lost every-thing...but her secrets. When the world catches up to them, will the price of their lies cost them everything?

Texas Healer: Special Forces medic holds the power to heal both a doctor's injured body and her wounded heart...but she can't stay in his world—and he can't leave.

Texas Protector: A detective forever haunted by the night when he couldn't save a young girl from trauma—now she's a cop herself and he has to send her undercover to lure a murderer.

Texas Deception: A plucky crusader falls for a down-on-his-luck stranger—only to learn too late that he's the villain determined to destroy her town

Texas Lost: A hard-nosed detective targeted by internal affairs and the woman who's professional evaluation will make or break his career. A a growing attraction between them risks first his case...and then her life.

Texas Wanderer: When she's lost all her dreams and is finally finding a place to call home, will she place her trust—and her heart—in the hands of a wanderer with secrets?

Texas Bodyguard: He's undercover as a bodyguard to a film star because her best friend is his top suspect. When she comes to mean too much to him, confessing his deception means risking his career—but not coming clean with her could risk her life

Texas Rescue: A haunted warrior who lives in the shadows encounters a small, valiant woman who's a champion of lost causes, and the vibrant light within her lures him from the darkness. When she is rocked by a brush with evil, can he make her feel safe again...and can she convince him that he deserves to live in the light?

* * *

About the Author

New York Times and *USAToday* bestselling Texas romance author of the popular TEXAS HEROES series and over 50 other novels in romance and women's fiction, a five-time RITA finalist and RT BOOKReviews Career Achievement Award winner, Jean Brashear knows a lot about taking crazy chances. A lifelong avid reader, at the age of forty-five with no experience and no training, she decided to see if she could write a book. It was a wild leap that turned her whole life upside down, but she would tell you that though she's never been more terrified, she's never felt more exhilarated or more alive. She's an ardent proponent of not putting off your dreams until that elusive 'someday'—take that leap now.

Connect With Jean

Visit Jean's website: www.jeanbrashear.com

Facebook: www.facebook.com/AuthorJeanBrashear

BookBub: www.bookbub.com/authors/jean-brashear

Pinterest: www.pinterest.com/JeanBrashear

Instagram: www.instagram.com/jeanbrashear

To be notified of new releases and special deals, sign up for Jean's newsletter on her website

CPSIA information can be obtained
at www.ICGtesting.com
Printed in the USA
BVHW080324290119
538933BV00001BA/19/P